THE OCEAN

JAMES HANLEY, novelist, short-story writer and playwright, was born in Dublin in 1901 and brought up in Liverpool. At thirteen, he ran away to join the Black Watch Battalion of the Canadian Expeditionary Force and fought in the First World War. He spent nine years at sea, and this profoundly influenced his writing. His second novel *Boy* (1931) was prosecuted for obscene libel, and this gave him a notoriety that may have led to the unjustified neglect of his powerful and startling work. He died in 1985, leaving a body of work which includes 31 novels.

James Hanley

THE OCEAN

THE HARVILL PRESS
LONDON

First published by Faber and Faber in 1941

This edition first published in Great Britain in 1999 by
The Harvill Press
2 Aztec Row, Berners Road
London N1 0PW

www.harvill.com

1 3 5 7 9 8 6 4 2

A CIP catalogue record is available from the British Library

ISBN 1 86046 675 3

Designed and typeset in Walbaum
at Libanus Press, Marlborough, Wiltshire

Printed and bound by Butler & Tanner Ltd
at Selwood Printing, Burgess Hill

To
Barbara and Walter
affectionately

THE OCEAN

I

WHEN THE LIGHT BROKE the sailor got up and looked about him. Clear sky, silent heaving masses of water. No other boats. Horizon's line a blur.

"Thank God for that," he said, and sat down.

It was a world from which his eyes shrank, a stupor of blue. He looked down the boat. In the prow a figure was sitting, quite still, the head bobbing about like a cork in water. At his feet a man lay flat on his back. One was in a half kneeling position, being sick over the side of the boat. Another was doubled up in sleep, snoring loudly. The sailor got up again and looked around. Then he went right aft. He saw a man lying face downwards in the bottom of the boat. Under him was the water keg.

"Poor Crilley," he said.

He dragged the body off the keg and carried it further amidships. Then he laid it in a more respectable position, took a piece of canvas and covered it. The body was riddled with bullets. He went back to his seat.

"Thank God for the light," he muttered to himself. Slowly he began to remember.

He was a short, stockily built man. He was wearing a reefer jacket, a pair of blue dungaree trousers, and a brown shirt

3

open at the neck. He was bareheaded and his thick black hair appeared matted on his head. Periodically he pushed his fingers through the mass, and scratched. They were distracted fingers. His grey eyes were almost hidden under the bushy brows, they were bloodshot and heavy-looking.

"I can't understand," he said, rising to his feet again, staring about him, his eye finally lighting on the heap under the canvas.

"Christ! They've gone," he said.

This time he slumped down heavily in his seat.

Silence was like mountains, stupid with power.

His hand went to his pocket and he took out his watch. Its smashed face showed five minutes past twelve.

"Of course! That's right. Shortly after midnight."

He remembered now. He had just turned into his bunk when there was a violent explosion aboard the *Aurora*, and immediately he had been flung out again. The syren was blowing. Grabbing his trousers and a coat he put them on, finally staggered with others through the now darkened fo'c'sle, and so to the welldeck. He slipped and fell, got up again and ran on towards his boat. The ship had listed. There were shouts and cries all about him. Somewhere on the starboard side he heard a loud crash. He knew his boat was not on the weather side. He bumped into a ventilator, finally found the companion ladder, grabbed, climbed, forced his way through a jabbering group shouting names. He began shouting orders then, and he saw the boat swung out. At the same moment the ship gave a great convulsive movement, the fall broke, a block screeched, he cried, "Look out there!" And then the boat was not there, but he was standing in the same place and many hands were dragging at him. He cried out to them. "Keep cool!"

4

Breaking free, he caught the swinging fall and vanished. A burning sensation in his hands and then he reached the boat. It was still upright. When he let go the rope his body went hurtling as the boat heaved, he staggered down half its length. He could see his outstretched hand, but no further than that.

"Damn!" he said, "damn."

Then he made his way to where the fall was dangling. He could not see the *Aurora*, but he sensed its toppling height, its dark mass, and high up what looked like shadows danced about where the boat had been.

"Down you come."

As each man came down he steadied himself, hung on to the rope, grabbed with his free hand the trembling bundle of a body, said, "Righto". One after another they came. It began to rain. A heavy head swell was running. He thought always of the boat smashing up against the plates of the *Aurora*. He thought always of the men coming down. He thought of a man named Crilley.

"Crilley!"

"Coming down."

He grabbed Crilley's legs, then the man darted away, his body held for a moment the electric throb of a caught fish. Then he was gone. Two more followed him. The rope swung lazily in the wind.

"Coming down," he cried at the top of his voice, "coming down."

He stood waiting there.

"Coming down," he cried, "coming down."

The rope still swung. Above there were many cries. The ship seemed quite still now, it was the darkness that lurched drunkenly.

5

"Any more?" he cried at the top of his voice, "any more?"

He moved slowly along the boat, touching bodies. All were shivering. He felt each body, said, "Are you all right now?"

Sounds came to his ears, mumblings, a groan, somebody being sick. He made his way back, bat-like to where the fall hung. He heard a dull roar, his mind cried, "Away, away."

He drew a sheath knife from his pocket and cut the rope. The boat rocked, her nose struck the bulk of the *Aurora*.

"Coming down," he cried, "anybody coming down?" He listened, he felt the rope. "No use," he said, and cut the other rope. The boat danced, it was free. He fell, sprawled, his hands groped, he dragged on an oar. He got up, pointed the oar, pushed hard against the *Aurora*'s plates.

"Away," his mind cried, "away, away."

He sensed the sucking power of water under his boat. He pushed with all his strength. Suddenly the boat was ablaze with light. "My God!" he said.

"Down, down," he shouted thickly. "Down." Bullets whistled past his head. His body clawed the bottom of the boat.

"Crilley, the water," he cried, "the water."

"O.K.," Crilley said.

The light went out, the darkness deepened. The sailor lay flat in the boat. He saw nothing, felt nothing, heard nothing. He lay still. All sound ceased. A wheel had been whirring in his head, and suddenly it had stopped. Silence. He lay waiting. After a few minutes he sat up, looked about, called in a squeaky voice, "Crilley." No answer.

"Crilley."

No answer.

"Cril-ley."

Silence.

"My God!" he said. "Crilley."

Quietness flowed into his mind, thoughts cooled, he sat very still. Rain went down his neck, drops hung on his nose. When he put his hand to his head, feeling his wet and matted hair, he exclaimed, "Hell! Where've I been? In the water? But how?"

He could not remember anything.

"Anybody hear me?" he called out.

Someone was sick, groaning.

"How many are you? Goddam open your mouths, you're not going to die."

"I'm all right."

"Who are you?"

"Benton's my name."

"Who else?"

"My name's Stone."

"Are you all right?"

"There's an old man sick down here," a voice said.

"Come here," the sailor said.

A figure came up and was grabbed.

"Sit down," the sailor said. "By me."

The man sat down.

"You're Stone?"

"No. Benton."

"Good! Here."

He pushed oars into the man's hands. "Row," he said, "I don't care how. Just row. Keep cool, everything will be all right."

Without quite realizing it he was rowing himself.

He remembered all this as he sat aft, looking at the figures in the boat, his eye noting the differing positions of the bodies. As the light grew they stood out more clearly. He counted them. Six. He stood up, stretching his arms, he yawned loudly, looked away towards the horizon. It spelt emptiness.

"Now I've got things to do," he said.

There was a man lying at his feet and the sailor touched him gently with his foot.

"What's your name?" he said.

The man opened his eyes and sat up. "Hell," he said, "it's cold."

Later he said, "I'm Stone," noting dark stubble on the sailor's chin.

"Good! All right, you can lie down again," the sailor said.

"What's your name?" asked the other.

"Me? Curtain. Joseph Curtain."

Then he went on to the next man. He was wide awake, lying awkwardly across a seat amidships.

"Which is Benton?" he said.

"I'm Benton."

"Are you all right? No bones broken; anything like that?"

"I'm all right," the man said, slumped back into his former position.

Curtain went for'ard. There was a man sitting in the bow of the boat, bareheaded, it bobbed about in a helpless sort of way with the movements of the boat.

"What is your name?"

When the head turned the sailor sat down and stared at the man. He was old.

"You're a priest," the sailor said, his tone of voice had changed.

"My name is Michaels, Father Michaels. I've been trying to remember what happened," he said, his child-like eyes full on Curtain's face.

"We were torpedoed at five minutes past twelve last night,

and later the boat was machine-gunned. The other sailor is dead. He's there," pointing to the heap under the canvas.

The old man shook his head. "How terrible – how dreadful," he said.

"Are you all right?"

"I've been sick," the priest said, "very sick. I feel much better now."

"Who is this man?"

They both looked at the long, thin figure of a man lying flat on his back.

"I can't tell you," Father Michaels said, "I can't –"

Curtain suddenly turned away, heard the old man being violently sick. He bent down and touched the man on the shoulder. He did not respond.

"Are you all right?" he said. "What is your name?"

The man opened his eyes. "Kay," he said, "oh, Kay." Then he closed them again. Curtain put a hand in his pocket and drew out some wet papers and looked through them. He then returned them.

"His name's Gaunt. John Gaunt."

He studied the figure at his feet.

"Has this man been sick?" looking directly at the old priest. Then he said, "I see." The old man had fallen fast asleep.

"Gaunt," Curtain said. "Mr. Gaunt's had a clout on the head."

Taking out a large handkerchief he dipped it in the sea, began wiping blood from the man's forehead. The eyes opened again.

He looked up at the sailor, bewildered.

"Your name's Gaunt, you've had a nasty knock."

"Kay, Ka-y," Gaunt said.

"Is your name Gaunt?"

9

"Kay," the man said.

The sailor turned away and went aft again. "There are things to be done," he said, "things to be done." He returned carrying a baler with some water in it. He knelt down, put a hand behind Gaunt's head, said, "Here! Drink this. You'll be all right soon."

He forced water down the man's throat, but Gaunt did not feel it, nor did he see Curtain bent over him. He saw only the seas that raced towards him, the seas parting, and then he went down. He was spread-eagled on the ocean bed.

"Where are you, Kay?"

He clawed for a hold, but great holes appeared, the ocean bed was cracking, the fissures were like great veins.

"Drink this," Curtain said, watching the drops of water trickle down, "You'll be fine soon."

There was no rest and no hold. The ocean's bed gave way, and he plunged.

"Kay," he said.

"Look at me, Gaunt," Curtain said. "You're all right. You've had a clout on the head. You'll be O.K. in a minute. Just lie there quiet, see."

There was a hollow whistling sound blowing about in Gaunt's mind, so that he could not hear the sailor's words. Darkness was a wall, towering, and he began to climb.

"Where are you, Kay?"

Curtain rolled up the man's coat sleeve, tore a piece from the sleeve of his shirt, tied it around Gaunt's head.

"You'll be all right, don't you worry. Lie quite still."

He left him, went down to where Crilley lay, and stood there looking at him.

"Poor Crilley," he said, sitting down, watching closely the canvas as though every second he expected to see it moving.

"One dead, one asleep, one light in the head. One horribly sick." He glanced at the man still being sick over the side of the boat.

One was sitting up now, staring at him.

"That must be the fellow Stone," he thought, got up and went along to him.

"You're Stone, aren't you?"

"I'm Stone," the man said.

"We are in an awkward position," Curtain said. "Have you got a watch?"

"No! Is that a man lying there?"

"Yes. A man named Crilley. They got him. We may be picked up soon."

"You really think so?"

"Why not?"

More cautiously he added, "Of course we might not. It's hard to say. I half believe they smashed the ship's wireless, we ought to have been picked up by now. We're some hundreds of miles from the land. I think the other two boats were smashed up. I thought there might be a sign of them when the light came. I was rowing a long time in the darkness."

"What happened to him?" Stone said, his finger pointing.

"He machine-gunned the whole boat. As soon as I saw the searchlight I knew he'd do that. That's nothing new. I was at the other end of the boat. It was bloody confusing I can tell you. Every minute I expected the boat to be turned over. Anyhow Crilley got it, he was on the water keg. I'd only just looked at it and hadn't even time to shove it back in the locker. No time for anything."

"But d'you suppose they knew he was lying on that keg?"

"Oh, I don't know," Curtain said, a sigh in his voice, a grudge there. "It's one of those things that makes a man think. Crilley was my mate aboard the *Aurora*. When they machine-gun a boat like this there's always a chance of them drilling holes in your water supply. These days they don't kill you directly, but if you plug a water keg with bullets then you kill every-body – in the best German manner. After all I've only one way of looking at it. We may be picked up to-day. But if we're not we can't keep the man under that canvas. You're not scared or anything?" and he looked directly into the other's eyes.

"No," Stone said, "I'm not scared."

"Good! Now you just sit there quiet till I come back. I'm going to have a look round, and I won't be long."

Stone looked out at the ocean. "It's enormous," he said. He did not know how long he had been staring at it, but Curtain came back and he turned round.

"Not feeling sick or anything?" Curtain said, and sat down by him.

"A lot of things must have happened when the boat crashed," Curtain said. "Still, one can't complain. We've got oars. Can you row?"

"I'll try."

"Good! There's water, a tin of biscuits and three tins of milk. I'll go the round of you fellers turning out your pockets," he said, forcing a smile. "I threw matches overboard that weren't matches any more. There should have been other things. You make all sorts of preparations for these events, and then when the thing happens you begin to wonder if it hasn't all been a bloody waste of time. Still, no grumbles, we've got the things to shift the boat along, we've some food. That's the most important. So long as every man keeps cool, keeps a hold on himself, I'm satisfied. I'm the only sailor in the boat. You're all strangers to me. But I shall have to rely on every one of you, except that old priest for'ard. He is useless. I'll set watches, each man takes his turn at the oars. Taking no chances I'll ration each man with a biscuit and some water. I'll keep the milk for a tea party."

At that moment Stone groaned, leaned over the boat, was sick.

"That's good," the sailor said. "Get it over."

He gripped Stone's shoulder with one hand; pressed the other flat on the man's forehead.

"That's it," he said, "get it all up." He then pulled the man, let him rest against his shoulder, looked down at the other men, suddenly forgot Stone, ceased to feel his weight on him. He was staring at the old priest, at Gaunt flat on his back. Slowly his head moved round, smoothly, like something on a well-oiled swivel, he was searching the waters. But he could see nothing, and the silence grew.

"Now are you all right?" he asked, looking at Stone, whose face was half ashen, half green. "Feel better now?"

Stone's lips moved but no words passed between them.

"Oh hell," Curtain muttered.

He made the man comfortable, propped up against a seat, then went amidships. He stood there looking at the others. He did not speak to them. He spoke to Crilley under his breath.

"I wish you were here," he said. "Poor old Crilley."

He put his hands to his eyes, searched the skyline, mumbling to himself, "Out of a ship, and out of a job. In your bunk one minute, in the bloody ocean the next. That's how it is."

Saying this he slid, went down on one knee, then the other, leaned on the seat. He fell asleep that way.

II

HE HAD A LITTLE BOOK with a canvas back, and he opened it, taking out a stub of pencil. On the front page it read, "To Dad from Nell." He wrote down the names in this book. Gaunt. Father Michaels. Stone. Benton. Crilley. He crossed the name Crilley out, "Unless we get picked up to-day," he said to himself. Then he put the book back in his pocket and went for'ard. Benton and the priest were sitting close together, talking. Gaunt sat near them, but he did not appear to be listening, there was a trance-like expression upon his face. Curtain saw how the piece of shirt had stuck to his temple. He thought he would not do anything about it yet. He sat down. The boat tossed crazily, wind came over the bow, blowing through the scattered grey hairs of the priest. Without turning round, Curtain called, "Stone." The others looked at him. He waited until Stone came up.

"Sit down," he said. "Every four hours I will issue a ration. Every four hours a man will take a turn at the oars. There's nothing to worry about. That's all," he said, and his eyes wandered from man to man.

"D'you think we'll be picked up to-day?" Benton asked.

"I can't say that," the sailor said. He looked away from them.

The ocean was big, the boat was small, he wished he had another sailor in the boat with him, it would make all the difference. He was a complete stranger amongst these men, he did not know them, they him. "I soon will, though," he reflected.

"What are you going to do with the man down there?" inquired Stone.

"Unless we get picked up to-day, bury him," Curtain said.

There was a sudden silence. They looked anywhere but at each other. The ocean seemed to command their attention.

"It's strange we've not come across the other boats," Benton said, "but perhaps we might come on them later in the day."

"I keep thinking of that poor man," Father Michaels said.

"Are you better, Gaunt?" Curtain asked, leaning over, placing a hand on the man's knees.

"I'm better," Gaunt said, and Curtain saw a face drained white. It was so white one wondered if it had ever carried blood.

"You just sit quiet, Gaunt. That's all you have to do for the present. Stone, you come aft with me. Anybody got a watch? Mine shows five minutes past twelve, but it's been doing that for hours now." He stood up, waiting.

"I have," the priest said, his trembling fingers fumbling at his pocket.

"All right," the sailor said, and the next minute the old man's watch was in his hand. "You might lend me this."

"Take it," Father Michaels said.

The sailor left them, Stone following behind him.

"That chap Gaunt looks a bit odd to me," Stone said.

"He's had a knock on the head. He'll be as right as rain shortly."

"If I remember rightly there was a woman with him on the *Aurora*. It may have been his wife."

"Hard lines! But she's probably got away in one of the other boats. I don't recall seeing him on the boat, nor you for that matter. But then a sailor never sees the passengers on a ship until it's too damned late, and then he doesn't know half enough about them. Have you been in a position like this before?"

"No," Stone replied, "I haven't," but Curtain seemed not to hear him. He was measuring out water in a tin.

"Here," he said, "and the biscuits are as hard as hell. You don't have to eat it unless you want it, see?"

Stone took the cigarette tin of water and drank it at a gulp. There was something about the biscuit that deterred, he put it in his pocket. Curtain watched him do this, but he did not say anything.

He saw a man about thirty-five years of age, tall, well built, clean shaven, with sandy hair, already thinning about the temples. He had a long nose, and his mouth was small. He had brown eyes. Looking at him it gave the sailor a feeling of confidence. He wondered who he was, where he had come from. Later Stone told him that he came from the Midlands, but did not say where exactly. He was a teacher. He had been on his way out to a new job in Canada.

"I see," Curtain said, "I see. Now about the others. Hey there, Benton!"

Stone went away, stopped dead, said, "I'll row now."

"Yes, row," the sailor said. "I'll be with you in half a tick."

Benton came down.

"That chap Stone doesn't seem to like the look of the biscuits, neither do I. But I should say they were better than nothing, wouldn't you?" remarked Curtain, when Benton came up, smiling at the younger man, coaxing as he filled the tin with water and handed it to Benton.

"No more'n twenty," he thought.

"Have you ever been in a boat before?" looking at his slight build, his fair hair, and open, boyish face, at the same time noting that the young man had managed in some miraculous way to get clear of the *Aurora* with a suit and overcoat. There was something rather shy about Benton, too, he thought.

"I've rowed a boat on the Thames," Benton said. "I suppose you know all about boats, Curtain."

"Here y'are. Get it down. And here's your biscuit. You won't get anything else before midday. You can take the oars when you've had that. You don't look sick to me. That comes of rowing on the Thames," he concluded.

He waited for the tin, took it, and refilled it. Then he went for'ard to the old priest.

"Oh, no, no," Father Michaels said, at sight of the tin. "I can't, I – daren't. I'm –"

"You must drink this water all the same," Curtain said. "Can you eat the biscuit?"

He put an arm round the old man.

"You're wet, too. It seems odd to me, my hair's got oil on it. Perhaps we were in the water together. I can't remember anything very much."

He forced the tin to the priest's lips, but took it away quickly and turned to Gaunt. He heard Father Michaels being sick again.

"Here, Gaunt," he said, "you'll get another ration at midday."

Gaunt took the water and biscuit saying, "Thanks," but he did not look at the sailor.

"D'you suppose there's a chance of our sighting the other boats?" he questioned.

"I don't know. It all depends on the course they took. But I shouldn't worry. I feel certain we'll be found to-day."

"My wife was aboard the boat, too," Gaunt said.

"I heard something about it from the man Stone. I'm damned sorry about that, but I expect she'll turn up in one of the other boats."

"It doesn't matter now," Gaunt said, handing back the tin. He put the hard biscuit in his pocket.

"Something a bit queer about this fellow," thought Curtain. "I'll have to watch him. Can't take any damn chances. He's not fit to do anything, either."

He ruminated on Gaunt. "I'll let them keep each other company for a bit. Benton, Stone and myself can look after things."

He turned once more to the priest. "Feel better now?"

He wanted to say then that he was afraid they were going to run into some rough weather, thought better of it, said nothing.

As he left them, he leaned over Gaunt and said, "If you see a ship, shout, if you see *anything*, shout."

He found Stone seated and pulling well. Benton was behind him. He took up the oars and began to row.

For some time they rowed in silence. Curtain did not see the men in front of him, nor Gaunt. He did not see the old priest. He saw Crilley lying on the water keg. He wished that Jennins or Grimes had been in the boat with him. One saw strangers aboard the *Aurora*, but in this small boat men were stranger still. He thought how a sailor was faced with that sort of thing all his life. He talked to himself as he rowed. He hoped Jennins and Grimes had got away safely. They, with Crilley, had been his mates.

He saw Stone's oars suddenly drag water, "Pull them in," he said.

Benton went on rowing. "If he thinks he is rowing on the Thames, that is good," thought Curtain.

When he looked ahead he saw a blaze of light across the skyline. The light was hard, it hurt the eyes. He began to talk to them. Warmth grew between them. He thought how he could rely on these two men, and once he wondered whether the old priest would stand up to it. He was so old, sixty-eight or -nine, he thought, frail, like an old baby. Benton came from Somerset. He talked about it. His girl was there.

"You're getting tired, son. Pull in that oar."

He went on rowing. Stone talked about his home in the Midlands, his work there. He hoped he would get his job back again.

"I lost mine, too," Curtain said, laughing loudly, "a sailor's always changing his jobs. You don't get time to like them," he said.

Stone picked up the oars again.

Sometimes Stone dozed as he rowed, and when he opened his eyes the sky was yawning down at him, the ocean seemed twice as large, dizzying him.

"We shall be picked up to-day," he told himself. "We shall be picked up to-day. I'm certain of that."

His mind felt stronger under the thought, the boat seemed to shoot through the water. But it was only the hard, long, and steady pull of the sailor behind him that set the boat plunging forward, towards what seemed to Stone an ever receding skyline.

"What are you thinking about, all silent there, Stone?"

Benton's head was low, almost resting on the other's shoulders.

"Nothing," Stone said, whose head was already flooded with ships, hands waving, shouts across water, hands picking him up, safe, and a place to hide from sky and water that overpowered and made his mind reel. When they heard him being sick, Curtain told him to go aft and lie down for a while.

"I'm all right where I am," Stone said, being sick where he sat.

He could not move, his body seemed to have taken on added weight, there was a queer feeling at the pit of his stomach, the sky was beginning to tremble over him.

"You'll feel fine after that," the sailor said.

The oars screeched in the rowlocks. Benton had his oar out again, rowing hard, but Curtain knew that this would not go on for very long. He thought of a townee in the country trying to dig an acre in an afternoon. But he liked Benton, he was cheery, he was willing. A little bumptious, but that did not matter. So long as they talked, were amiable, everything would be fine. The silence of the ocean could not escape them, there was something not a little ominous about it, the dreary wastes of water surrounding. But there were things worse than that and Curtain knew them. Silence in the boat would be worst of all. With words one could build walls, shut out the ocean.

Benton started plying him with questions about the *Aurora*, saying he could not remember how he had come down the rope. He talked of the torpedo, the submarine, the bullets over the boat.

"We don't want to talk about that now," Curtain said, "already you're dead beat. I can see it. Go aft and lie down with Stone. It's a long pull. Sometimes you feel you're just pulling round in circles, but it's always the same in the first hours. Have you been sick yet?"

"I was sick last night," Benton said, turning round.

They faced each other now. For the first time Benton was seeing Curtain close, and there was something about the sailor that he liked.

He watched Curtain rowing, watched his hands, and he saw with what ease, with what precision the sailor rowed, humming to himself as his body swung to and fro. He kept looking at Curtain's hands, and now he could see them serving out the rations, sitting Gaunt up, holding on to Father Michaels' shoulder. They were large hands, browned, hairy, with short stub fingers. Looking at them he thought of iron, granite. With what certainty he rowed, as though always there was a ship hovering near the horizon. He thought then, "We depend on him."

Curtain tending them, cheering them up, watching them all. Talking to break down the silence of others. Curtain wiping slobber from the old priest's mouth, giving him a drink of water from the baler. Curtain was the plan working. He was the cause and the effect, the order and the hope, the plan and its achievement. Not hurried, not confused, believing, certain. All this was crystal clear to Benton as he sat there looking at Curtain's hands, and at his face, darker by a day's growth of beard, but behind it the same feeling of granite, rocks. When at last the sailor looked up he found Benton asleep, his body rocking with the boat.

"A good kid," Curtain said, "a good kid."

He drew in the oars, laid them, sat back, let the boat go. A slight wind was now behind them.

He looked at Benton, beyond him to Father Michaels and Gaunt, but he did not look at Stone, satisfied to hear him snoring.

"The dirty lot of bastards," he said, Crilley in his mind, Crilley suddenly appearing from under the canvas, Crilley rising up out of the sea, looking at him, water dripping from his clothes, his body full of bullets.

"I'll have to see his missus, too. Goddam," he said, "goddam."

It could have been that old man. Crilley was only thirty. "I wonder if it would've mattered?"

He saw Mrs. Crilley. Her name was Jane.

Curtain passed down a road of his life, and Crilley and Jane and he were together, all laughing at Buster Keaton. That was a long time ago.

"He's dead, and I've got something to do about that. In the name of Jesus Christ, how could they know Crilley was on the water keg? Poor Jane," he said.

The devil could see in the dark.

"But he would not know of Crilley." His mind was full of Crilley, dead under the canvas.

For'ard Gaunt suddenly shouted like one crazy. "Ka-ay."

But Curtain did not hear this, nor see Gaunt, thinking of his wife and two children. He hoped he would be home soon.

"If the bastard'd done it in the daylight it would have been more decent," he thought, remembering the darkness, and the figures staggering about, and the boat dancing, and the blaze of light. The wind in his ears, and the rope flying past his face. Five bundles of fear coming down, clinging, and falling away from him into darkness, and the boat on the point of upturning. And hell rooted up.

Without realizing it he was looking at his hands, palms upwards, a burn, the mark of the hot rope there.

"I'll have to bury Crilley if nothing happens to-day. They must have smashed our wireless, goddam they would."

A great stretch of water darkened, he watched this, then looked up. A cloud shaped like a fist passed across, he thought he felt a raindrop on his face.

"Rain," he said, "rain."

He thought, "Rain, that's good," shivering now in his damp clothes. "I'll rig up something for the water."

He got up to go aft, but something in the attitude of the old priest made him pause. Father Michaels had his back to him, and his overcoat – "How the hell do they manage to remember overcoats?" – was thrown about his shoulders like a cloak, flapping in the wind. It made Curtain think of a large sea-bird, just alighted in the bow of the boat. But it was not this, only the way the old man's body seemed to be leaning, dangerously out over the bow. Was Father Michaels being sick again? He went up to him. Gaunt stared, a surprised look on his face, as though he had never seen the sailor before, but Curtain ignored the look, went to the priest and caught his arm.

"Are you sick?"

"He's fast asleep," Gaunt said. "He's been fast asleep for a week now."

"I didn't know that," Curtain said, thought quickly, "What the hell's wrong with this fellow?"

"How's your head, Gaunt?"

"Fine. It's better now. D'you think the old chap'll die?"

"I dunno, I dunno," Curtain said quickly, then turned and left him.

He searched about in the locker aft, found what he wanted. He thought there might be enough spare canvas to make some sort of shelter aft, if only to put the old man under it. The old man might die, he might not. Why had Gaunt asked that? Suppose the old priest had heard him.

"He's certainly sick," he told himself, then aloud, and angrily, "Goddam, they're all a bit queer. I wish Jennins was here. I wish Grimes was."

He flung down the piece of canvas and went to look at Crilley. He went resolved, put his hand down to pull away the covering, hesitated, "Poor sod," he said, "poor old Crilley," jerked it, saw a stiff hand, "no, not now," he said.

Passing Stone he kicked him gently. "Wake up there, Stone."

"What's the matter?"

"Nothing. I want to talk to you, that's all. The kid there is deado. Gaunt and the old man are no use to me at the moment. Sit up here and listen to me."

Stone yawned, said, "My ribs, my damn ribs."

"Your ribs are all right," the sailor said. "There's a man under that canvas and we've got to bury him. There are reasons why I think we ought to bury him to-night. Father Michaels is a very sick man, in spite of his general cheeriness. Exposure knocks them flat. Gaunt, I'm a little suspicious of since he got that bang on the head. A little thing like burying a chap might affect their nerves. It's bloody awkward, I can tell you. You got to sweat every nerve, you got to keep things going normal. Now tell me this," leaning over Stone, one hand pressed on his knee. "Would you be afraid – I mean, would you be a bit scared about helping me to stitch him up. I've canvas here. Some time after dark. Or d'you think we ought to have a proper ceremony, with the old priest here?"

"He knows there's a man dead aboard," Stone said, not thinking of Crilley, not thinking of Father Michaels, or remembering exactly what Curtain had been saying to him, his mind a little afraid, guessing, wondering.

"Everybody knows. I told them that unless we were picked

up to-day I'd put Crilley over. It's the only sensible thing to do. He was my mate."

The momentary silence was awkward, Stone was thousands of miles from Crilley, Curtain near to him, thinking of Jane, of a road in their lives, thinking of Crilley laughing at Keaton, dead on the water keg, Jane waiting.

"I wonder how Mum and Nell are," his mind said, his mind cloaking Nell, covering her, his mind seeing Mum, coming towards him, smiling. He always called her "Mum".

"Well," he said, "D'you think you'd be scared about stitching a sailor up, helping me with the job?"

"I'll help you," Stone said, "I'm awfully sorry. I didn't know he was your mate."

Curtain made no answer. There seemed no reason for doing so. Crilley was already gone, out of mind. Before he had talked of this burial, Crilley was still there, dead, but still close to him. Now he was gone, clean from his mind. Gone with Jane down another road, shadows at the end.

"All right, that'll do for me, then," he said, and went back to his job.

Rain fell heavier now. The light was beginning to go, something like a black cloth was beginning to spread across the sky. It began to pour. He found more spare canvas, an iron bar, two lengths of wood, a sea anchor, a coil of rope, an old heaving line. And as he picked them up and examined them they were already securing the man under the canvas.

"I wonder if any of those fellers has a cigarette."

"Crilley would come into this boat, too," he reflected, "the bloody fuss there was about the boat numbers," he said loudly, making Stone turn round.

"You haven't such a thing as a cigarette," Curtain said. Stone shook his head. "Hell, I wish I had," thinking, "now how the devil can he think I'd have cigarettes." He thought the question stupid.

"I wonder how long we'll be in this confounded position?" Stone said.

"Maybe a day, maybe a month, you can't tell," the sailor said, turning his back on him.

He knew how difficult it was for a man to keep his nerves. They were only a few hours in the boat as yet. Men got like that. It wasn't the first time he had been in an open boat.

"I got to watch the bloody lot of them," he thought. Watch every move. Every look, listen to every word. They had to keep their nerve. Again he wished Jennins or Grimes was with him. He did not know these men, worlds away from him. When finally they were picked up, they would go their way. He would never see them again. He had to trust them. They had to trust him. Everything would be all right so long as they held together, didn't get on one another's nerves, didn't growl, didn't always ask the same questions. You would be picked up or you would not be picked up. That was how it was. You got what was coming to you.

"Listen, Stone, I'm dead beat. Can I rely on you while I bunk down for an hour. You see when night comes I'll have to be on my bloody toes. If I can rely on you, then it's O.K."

"Of course," Stone said, "I'll wake you if we sight anything."

"That's good, that's fine."   .

He stretched out and covered his face with his hands. He looked at the sky through his fingers. After a few minutes Stone saw the hands fall away from the face. Curtain was asleep. He looked down at the sailor.

"He's well away, been rowing like hell. I'll go for'ard and

have a talk with them," hoping he would sight something, be the lucky one to cry out, "Ship! Ship!"

He found Gaunt sitting there, idly looking out over the seas, twiddling his fingers, playing with a piece of string. He heard Stone coming, swung round.

"He's asleep still. Been asleep a whole week," Gaunt said, pointing to the priest.

Stone ignored the remark, asked how he was feeling. Was his head any better.

"I'm all right now," Gaunt said. "That silly fool back there thinks I'm ill."

"Which fool?"

"That chap Curtain. Coming up here giving all kinds of orders."

"All right," said Stone, "don't shout it all over the damned boat." He could not fathom Gaunt. At that moment the old priest turned slowly round. He saw Stone. Immediately Gaunt got up and went away.

"What's the matter with him?" Stone asked the priest.

The old head shook, the hands on knees trembled, he opened his mouth, he might have been waiting to catch a fly. Stone thought he looked funny.

"You've been sick, too," he said, clasping his hands, drawing nearer to the old man.

"Yes. We've all been sick" – pause – "it will do us good the sailor says."

"He's a good chap."

"Yes. I wonder when we're going to be picked up. I've been trying to remember the things of last night. It's like a nightmare to me. I feel sorry for that man Gaunt. His wife was aboard the ship, I believe. I recollect seeing him with a woman on more than one occasion. But I'm not good at observing people."

He smiled slowly, "Though I should take more notice than I do. I'm getting old. Poor Gaunt got a bang on his head, from one of the ropes, I'm told."

"He's not very civil to people." Stone said.

"No! But he has something on his mind. He was telling me something about himself. He is a business man, in a big way, a concern in Scotland. He was going out to Canada with his wife. They have a son there. He seems to have had some trouble with his wife. Very sad for him, he doesn't know what's happened to her. I sympathized with him, and then he struck me as being a little callous about it all. I expect it's the effect of the knock on his head, and all the horror of his wife holds him down. I was trying to say my prayers earlier on this morning, but I found it most difficult. He talked the most utter nonsense to me."

"That's what made you sick, Father Michaels," said Stone, laughing, but the priest could not see the reason for this.

"How extraordinary it is to find ourselves sitting here like this, in a small boat, possibly hundreds of miles from land, and nothing to look on but the ocean."

Stone thought the old man looked tired, weary. He wondered how long Father Michaels would keep up the pretence. He was far from well.

"D'you know that man Gaunt has been wandering about the earth for the past ten years or so, he and his wife together, their home broken up, their son away in Canada. I feel sorry for him."

Stone was silent. He studied the white face, the puckered, trembling mouth. He looked at the collar on the old man's neck, at the black cloth suit, the overcoat almost green with age. Practical, he told himself that the collar must come off at once, it seemed far too tight, the old man might choke. But he was curiously shy, and would not mention it. Father Michaels had suddenly turned his back on him.

"You're very tired," Stone said. "Curtain is making a place for you, down there. You want to get a good long sleep. Can I get you anything? Would you like a drink of water?"

The head shook. He wanted nothing except to be left alone, and his head bobbed about in the air, as if it were something quite apart from his body.

Hearing loud noises Stone realized that Curtain was awake. Gaunt had woken him up. Gaunt was asking Curtain for a drink of water.

"In half an hour, Gaunt, not before," Stone heard Curtain say. "I thought I explained to you all. The water here is not for people to drink the moment they feel thirsty."

Stone got up, went down and joined them. "That's not long to wait, surely," Curtain said. "You won't die. I know you've had a rotten time, we all have. All are equal in this boat. You might as well go and sit down. When you feel a bit better you can take a hand – at the oars," concluded Curtain.

"I've rigged up a shelter there," he said, motioning Stone to come closer. "I want you to help me carry the old man along here. He thinks he can sit up there for ever, but he can't."

He pushed Gaunt out of the way. They went for'ard and picked up the priest. He uttered no word, hardly appeared to realize that he was being moved at all. They made him comfortable under the canvas.

"We'll have to watch that man Gaunt," Stone said. "He seems a weak creature."

Laughing, the sailor said loudly, "I'll watch you all." Gaunt sat with his head in his hands. They did not speak to him. Slowly he was remembering.

He was standing under the poop, the log wheel spinning below him, watching the white threshing ribbon of the *Aurora*'s wake, his body swaying with the movement of the ship, his ear attuned to the throb of engines below. He was looking out into the darkness, but there was no water there. Nothing except towns and cities reeling past. He thought of ten years of waste. He thought of Kay lying reading in her cabin, wondered if she had sent the wireless message to Denis. When the explosion came he was flung to the deck, his mind was full of Kay, and he staggered up, ran through the darkness, back to Kay. He remembered that. It was like a slow moving film, sometimes it stopped, then shot forward again, its speed crazy, everything was shadows, blurs. His mind was flooded by her. The deck was shuddering. After a while it was still. He reeled drunkenly, the *Aurora* had a list of nearly forty degrees. He ran on towards the cabin, stumbling in the blackness, crying, "Kay". Wind blew, other voices filled the air, there were screeching sounds. A light came on and vanished again. He bumped into a ventilator, swore loudly. "Kay, where are you, Kay?" He sprawled in the alleyway, dizzily climbed a ladder. He shouted through cupped hands, "Kay."

Somebody bumped into him saying, "Christ!" He stumbled over the steps of the cabin, in pitch darkness groped, dragged at bedclothes. "Kay! My God, where are you, Kay?" dragging the contents of two bunks to the deck. He ran out, blindly, shadows sailed past him. He felt something hard strike his head, a rope whizzed past his face.

"Where are you, Kay? Where am I?" hands to his head, standing dead still upon the deck. Everything was running amok.

Feet, tackle, planks, rope, coils, tarpaulins, everything was scattering about him.

"Where am I?"

A hand clutched his arm. "Which boat?"

"I don't know –" he had tried to break away, but his body was already moving, being dragged.

"Let me go! Where are you, Kay?"

"The ship is sinking," the quiet voice said, the other hand clutching.

"You're choking me, let me go – Ka-ay," shouting, half crying, "Kay!"

Bodies milled past, the ship heaved again, a light flashed, and then he saw her. He broke away, knocking the other to the deck, shouting to her, crying, "Kay, I'm here, Kay. My God, Kay."

She was in a boat, standing, clinging to a fall.

"Blast you, let me go," he shouted, another hand grabbing at him.

Was it Kay? Wasn't it Kay? Was she in the boat?

He thought she turned, hearing him, thought she cried, "John".

Did she cry "John"? He thought he was gripping her. He screamed, "Kay! Kay!" at the moment the light of a lamp went out, at the moment the boat was lowering. He flung himself to the deck. "Kay, Kay!"

"She's there! In the boat – my wife."

On all fours he crawled through forests of legs. Water poured along the deck, somebody picked him up.

"Grab the rope!"

He grabbed and the rope was Kay, clinging, "Kay! Kay!"

The words went out into the darkness. Somebody was lashing him to a rope.

"Hold on!"

"My God! Kay!"

He went whirling through space.

He fell in a heap, touching other bodies. When he woke up he was lying in the bottom of the boat. Two men were rowing. He sat up, stared about him. They were in the ocean. Ocean as far as he could see. There was no other boat. White and shaking he stared at the men, bewildered. The others were watching him. An old priest was near him, sitting with hands clasped on his knees, an old man being sick. Somebody said, "That man is ill."

Gaunt sat quite still and let the film whirl past. He did not raise his head, and the others did not speak to him. The hollow wind began blowing in his mind again.

III

"YOU NEEDN'T ROW UNLESS you want to," Curtain said. "Are you all right?"

"I'm all right," Gaunt said, "you let me row."

Benton was for'ard keeping a look-out. Father Michaels had not yet appeared from under his canvas shelter. Stone, Curtain, and Gaunt were sitting amidships. Stone kept staring at Curtain, and woodenly the sailor stared back at him. Gaunt took up oars and began rowing. After a while Stone, too, rowed. He noticed that the bandage was now gone from Gaunt's head. He noticed the stubble thicker, darker on Curtain's face, the eyes were half-closed. For some time they rowed without a word being spoken. Once or twice Benton turned round and looked at them, but he had nothing to say. Gaunt had slept most of the night.

When the darkness came Curtain had sent Benton for'ard. With Gaunt sleeping soundly and the priest out of sight, Curtain and Stone had gone about their business. And at the last moment Stone had drawn back. When Curtain looked at him now, he knew it was the Stone to whom he had stood so close, to whom he had said, "Are you afraid, Stone?"

Stone thought of it now. Of the extreme sense of loneliness

that had seized him, when together they had tied up Crilley after Curtain had carefully inserted the iron bar, of how they had carried the weight to the stern of the boat and laid it down. He had hedged then.

"We ought to wake up the priest," Stone said, "it's not right."

"I know how you feel on that score," Curtain said, "but you'd want me to get a very sick man from the shelter, and ask him to stand here in the wind and rain, saying prayers over this man?"

"It's horrible to me," Stone said, "I think we ought to get him up. It'll look quite different. You see – I mean –"

"I could say a prayer over him," Curtain said, "he was my mate. I know a prayer I could say."

Stone looked down at the bundle. It was drizzling rain, but he did not notice it. He was shivering violently and Curtain noticed this.

"You're shivering, Stone. How'd you expect me to get that poor old man up, sick as he is. Look here, you needn't do anything. I promise you. You just stand there quietly, that's all."

"But surely –" Stone said, a little frightened, slight desperation in his tone of voice.

"Listen to me," Curtain said, "I don't know whether you realize it or not, but I had better tell you that we are in a very serious position. We have a man with us who seems a little queer in his head. We've a bit of a youngster, we've an old, sick man. We don't know how long we'll be in this boat, like this, and personally I'm not in favour of another burial, and that's what you're asking for, Stone. I understand your feelings, I'm not a thick man, but I've got a certain responsibility, and if anything happens to any of you, it's me who'll have to do all the talking when the time comes. I don't think you understand as you say you do. Suppose Gaunt woke up and heard us, suppose Benton came running down here and saw what was happening. I don't want to be left in a boat with people who lose their nerve. It's too dangerous."

"I don't care," Stone said. "The priest's there, he ought to be waked up."

He was furiously stubborn. He would not listen to Curtain.

"This is none of your business," Curtain said, anger rising in him.

He wanted to cry, he did not know why. "Go to hell," he said. Crilley was in his mind, filled it, there was no place for Stone there. "Go away," Curtain said.

Stone did not move. He thought Curtain was not angry, only terribly calm.

"I don't want to lose my nerve," Curtain said, his voice lowered. "I'm no different to any of you. Why argue about burying a dead sailor? What can he mean to you?"

"I'm sorry," Stone said.

Curtain did not answer. He was bent down, his two hands gripping the lower part of Crilley's body. His lips moved, but no sound came from them.

"Don't you look back, Stone," he said.

There was a splash then, and Stone shuddered, but Curtain was quite still, looking at the dark, flowing water, listening.

"It's all over," he said. "Now you can go and sleep."

He left Stone standing there, went and picked up the oars, rowed alone. Stone did not move, but kept his eyes on the swift running waters, until feeling a little dizzied he sat down.

"How calm he is," he thought, "how calm."

They were in a serious position. Good God! Suppose they were never picked up? What would happen then?

He went along to where Curtain was sitting, gripped his hands so hard that the man stopped rowing.

"I was afraid," he said, "I was –"

"That's all right," Curtain said. "Forget it. We're all the same, we're all afraid, though some show it quicker than others. He was my best mate, been with me on the *Aurora* for years, been on other ships, too. We went everywhere together. He was only a bit of a lad. He's gone now, so what's the use of talking about it?"

"We might sight something to-day," Stone said.

"I'm taking no chances," Curtain said, "And I don't want to talk about this any more."

Nothing was so depressing to Stone as the boat when slowly the early morning light had seeped into it, giving shape to Gaunt and Benton, and the tired face of Curtain, the line of misery on faces more sharp and defined, the cold, clammy feeling that passed through him as his eyes wandered from end to end of the boat. He told himself that never in his life had he been seized with such a feeling of utter loneliness. Always the sailor was watching him, too. Watching him, as he watched the others.

Curtain's look was that of a man who expects nothing less than the improbable, nothing less than the reverse of normal in the acts of men.

"Why d'you keep looking at me like that?" Stone asked.

The sailor laughed. "Why the hell shouldn't I look at you?"

"There's the old man sick again," he said, "go and see to him." He watched Stone go.

"I wouldn't trust one of these people," he told himself, "not a man of them," remembering the argument with Stone in the night.

"My God! Scared of a poor dead man. Aye, and he'd be scared of a poor dead priest, too, if I'd listened to him, taken any notice at all. All nervy, that's what you have to watch."

He could hear Stone talking to Father Michaels, whose head now peered out from under the canvas, looking towards him.

"Morning, Father," he shouted.

"Gaunt, you and Stone carry the old man for'ard and make him comfortable. He likes to sit there, I know. Must be kept in the fresh air." Then he went on rowing, and after a while the three men passed him, and he smiled up at the priest, but when Stone whispered in passing that something had happened to the water, Curtain dropped his oars, said, "Damn and blast," and immediately went aft to see what had happened. He had a horror of anything happening to the water. Had somebody been at it? After the promises that had been made. And then he saw how wrong he was.

"Goddam," he said, staring at the canvas container he had rigged up. There was no water in it, and most of the night it had rained. He examined the keg. That was all right. Much relieved he went for'ard. He sent Benton away to lie down, saying, "How'd you feel this morning, son?" to which Benton replied, "Lousy," and went off.

Gaunt and Stone returned to the oars. Curtain sat down by the priest.

"Feel better this morning?" he asked, "breakfast time soon."

Father Michaels looked out over a grey, choppy sea, whirling clouds.

"I feel much better," he said. "I hope I won't be sick again. It makes me feel horrible. Don't bring me a biscuit, I can't eat them."

"I've something better than biscuit this morning. Milk."

37

"Would you think I was frightened if I told you I was very worried, I mean about our being seen, picked up?"

"I'm a little that way myself. Nothing to be ashamed of," Curtain said.

"I wasn't worrying very greatly about it," the priest said.

"I think you're fine," Curtain said. He leaned closer still.

"You ought to have those clothes off as soon as we get the sun. That won't be long. We're heading for the traffic lanes. May be found soon."

The eyes brightened, "But you're not quite certain of that, are you?"

"No," the sailor replied.

He wondered whether the priest would ask about Crilley, if he had noticed that the canvas bundle had gone. But the old man gave no hint of this. He turned his back on Curtain, his head began to bob.

"Actually counting the waves, I believe," Curtain muttered, smiling.

"I suppose you men are used to this sort of thing. I've been thinking much while sitting up here."

But Curtain did not answer him, for he was gone, back to Stone and Gaunt. He watched Gaunt rowing, thinking how odd it was that the man had so little to say. Even Benton and Stone had noticed it. There was a link missing in the chain that would bind them closer together. Often he wanted to mention this to Gaunt, but when his mind was full of it, he retreated. He told himself that the man had something on his mind, and it was useless to forge a link in the chain. Gaunt was ill now, rowing, lying, but Curtain thought him a clumsy liar. Then, before he quite realized it, he had said it.

"I'll tell you something, Gaunt," he said. "Benton and Stone

38

here, even Father Michaels, have noticed how silent you are. You've had a nasty clout, you got something on that mind of yours. This is a little boat, there are only five of us in it, and when one man is silent the others are bound to notice it."

"My mind's all to hell," Gaunt said, "I was worrying about something, about –"

He looked at Curtain, at Stone, then beyond them.

So the ocean shrank, the sky was a mere pencil line in space, the low screech of the rowlocks ceased, Father Michaels did not exist, Benton could not be seen, only the face of Gaunt. And they were sorry for this man. Something rose in them together, went out to Gaunt. They saw his face. In that moment there was nothing else to see.

"I heard about that," Curtain said, "I mean your wife. I'm sorry, but I expect she got safely away in one of the other boats."

And Stone said, "It must have been a terrible time for you."

Curiosity rising in him, he wanted to add, "How did it all happen?" but the expression on Gaunt's face said No.

"How long are we going to be like this?" Gaunt questioned.

Curtain glanced at Stone. "It's not desperate," he said quietly, let an oar drag, began scratching himself.

"Something tells me we'll be sighted to-day," Stone said, and quickly Curtain cut in, continued on from that, explained.

To-day the seas and oceans were not different to towns, cities, houses sprawling in valleys. Ships were over all the oceans to-day, in all the lanes of sea. One was not lost, never really lost. Always eyes were watching out for them. He said this looking directly at Gaunt. He talked then of ships, of many voyages he had been, of how he had spent most of his life at sea, except for a little schooling.

39

"The great thing is to have something to look forward to," Curtain said.

Like an electric wave these words passed into Stone's mind, scattered the fog of loneliness there.

"You just have to have patience," the sailor said, "keep cool, control yourself. Never give up hope. I learned to be like that, and I haven't lost much by it."

He talked of his wife and child, saying he expected to see them soon. So talking about them the ocean came back again, and they were walking grey waters towards him, smiling, and he saw them.

The boat shot forward under a fresh spurt of energy from Curtain.

The other two men did not notice this, they would not understand.

Mum's hand on Curtain's hand, Nell's hand. He rowed strongly, there was no ache or grind in it, he was thinking of his home, Nell laughing. Stone looked ahead, his hand heavy on the oars. To him it was like rowing towards eternity.

"Benton says he thought he saw a light last night," Curtain said, "but I think he was dreaming, I saw no bloody light. Did you, Stone?"

Stone said, "No," speaking as though from a great distance, inattentive, he was watching waves break, spray shoot into the air, far out battalions of white horses galloping. He watched the designs waves made, the sharp outline of the bow against them. He wondered what the normal world would be like when he got back to it. Houses, stones, voices, people walking in streets. Sometimes he imagined he saw a ship, wanted to shout, "Ship! Ship!" but in the dark fastness of his mind the ship was safely anchored in fevered waters. At times a feeling of weariness would seize him, leaving him limp, helpless. It was the immensity of the ocean, to which there seemed no end, no beginning.

With the automatic movement of a puppet his body swayed backwards and forwards, and sometimes the whole weight of the sea appeared to pile on the end of his oar. He never rowed more than an hour. Curtain knew this, wisely sent him away to lie down.

Gaunt had little to say, his mind was far away, he made some comments on the weather, surprising them, once remarked that he had nearly been drowned in a lake. But of what passed aboard the *Aurora* on the night of the disaster he had nothing to say. They left well alone, not questioning him. The *Aurora* was gone, meant nothing, the ship that should sight them was everything.

"You'd better give it up, Gaunt," Curtain said at length, after what seemed a long silence. "You think you're O.K., but you're not. Go and lie down."

He got up and went for'ard. They saw him sit down by the priest.

"Queer bird," Stone said.

"Nerves, a bit scared, a bit selfish perhaps," Curtain replied.

"D'you think the old man will last out, he's very weak?"

"I'm no oracle, why ask me, I can't tell you that."

A quietness came over the boat. Curtain could hear the rhythmic lap-lap of the water against the sides of the boat. The sound of oars moving was a gentle whirring in his mind.

When Stone looked at him some minutes later he exclaimed, "Good Lord!" Curtain was fast asleep, and he was rowing. Stone pulled in his oars and laid them down. Then without waking Curtain, he drew them from the man's hands. Then he went on rowing. Once or twice the sailor's head bobbed violently. Stone's arms began to ache. For'ard Gaunt was still talking to the priest.

Time sank. There were long, misty periods for Father Michaels, during which his body lolled lazily to and fro with the rhythm of the boat, when he was barely conscious of its movements. Body and mind were separated, and the mind moved slow, ponderous, like the ocean itself. Men would come by him but he would not see them, nor hear their movements. They were like his thoughts, vague, dream-like. His mind hung always on the threshold of sleep. Curtain had said that he looked like a baby sitting up in its cot, staring in wonderment at the sea. The murmur of the ocean floated into his mind like fog. His ears were flooded with sounds like music. The lapping water against the boat, under the bows gentle sounds like sobs. Wind came over the bow, made hollow, whistling sounds in his ears. Wind blew through his scattered grey hairs, but he did not feel it, and the cold, shivering feeling that sometimes made him feel sick would vanish. Between fitful dozes the scene would alter, sky and water change shape and colour. Once he opened his eyes and sky and water were no longer there, he lay in a world of air, through which there filtered the low, whistling sounds that filled his ears. Somewhere at the back of his mind there was a loch, and in it reeds stirred in the silent water. The sky would be of many colours, white and grey, black like pitch, a fiery red, once a blazing green. His head bobbed about, seemed to live independently of the rest of his body, so that he was not conscious of wet clothes, nor the odour that rose from them, unconscious of the collar, wet and shrunk and yellowed on his neck, that now held a tighter grip there,

cutting into his skin. Nor would he feel the nausea that precip-
itated the bouts of vomiting. His mind was like a cradle,
rocking gently in the sea.

Dream and actuality were separate only by the hair's breadth,
he would sit up shivering, feeling this, where but a moment
ago he had been floating face downwards upon a sea whose
surface carried the cunning of great silent lakes. He would feel
with trembling fingers, flung into the trough of the wave that
first had carried him mountain high. There were moments
when the ocean was only the quiet winding river over which
he crossed in a small boat, rowed by one youth in a white sur-
plice, and he was seated holding the Host, and watching for
the moment when the boat would touch the bank. Quiet and
unrest were the varying winds that rocked the cradle in which
he lay. Once he thought of the *Aurora*, there was a momentary uproar in his mind, then the ship vanished. Slowly his
head would sink down on his breast and he would sleep.

Sometimes thoughts were not vague, but took definite shape,
and he would watch the movements of waves, hearing far off
the cries of birds, the lonely curlew hovered fugitively above
his church, outside of which the congregation stood waiting for
him, children in front carrying flowers in their hands, the men
and women behind wearing their Sunday best, waiting for him
to come and lead them to the water's edge where the boats lay,
awaiting the blessing of his uplifted hand. All sounds were
music to him, and he would sit listening to these sounds. At
times everything was so still that the noise of the rowlocks
became thunderous to him, beating like wings against the
quietness of his mind.

When darkness came Curtain would go along and make
him comfortable for the night. He would say, "Thank you, Mr.

Curtain," making the sailor smile, for no other man addressed him thus. He would not see Curtain, nor feel his body being moved, nor the canvas wrapped about his feet, he heard only the voice saying, "Are you all right now?"

As the darkness grew he watched the sky, beholding the strange movements and shapes of clouds, some low and ominous-looking, others thin like threads stretching across the white background. Sometimes he saw great sheaves of slow-moving cloud, darkening large stretches of sea. A star would come out and he would throw back his head, look up and watch it. He thought of a single candle lighted in the dark desert. With the coming of a second star, and a third, his mind broke free once more, he left his inert body in the boat, and went wandering away, half buried thoughts sluggishly stirring, then clear pictures forming, passing across its surface, taking definite shape.

There were no stars and no sky, only a boy lighting candles on the altar of his church in Ireland, which was not so far away, just outside his boat, he had but to step into this church, it was so near to him, the warm, close smell of incense in his nostrils. He would walk through the aisles of quiet towards the mass of light, kneel down and pray. The shapes grew as the darkness deepened, he could touch these things with his hands. When the pictures vanished he saw a wilderness of dark, glimmering water, cold-looking when stars came out. It made him think of a pale light slow moving over a great field of ice. Sometimes the sound of voices was no different to the sound that wind and water made. They were one, fused. The monotonous movement of oars, the steady whir-whir of the rowlocks died away. Once his mind was Christ filled, he saw Him walk these waters.

IV

"ARE YOU ASLEEP?" Gaunt said.

"No, no! Go on, I can hear you," Father Michaels said.

"Something about Kay," the priest said.

There were moments when Gaunt would suddenly cease talking, forget the old man was there, listening. There were blanks in the narrative, in Gaunt's mind, like railway stations, dark, deserted, wind-blown.

"Oh yes," he said, "Kay."

Father Michaels was looking at him now, mouth trembling, water coming from his eyes.

"I'm sorry for you, Mr. Gaunt. But I would not give up hope," he said, and the words trailed away like smoke, "would not give up hope."

"Hope," Gaunt said, watching the old man whose name he could never remember, watching him groping in the pocket of his damp, greenish overcoat for a handkerchief. He dabbed his face with it, stuttered something from behind its folds, "Hope on, Gaunt," then dabbed frenziedly at one eye, an elusive drop defied the handkerchief. "Hope on," Gaunt said.

You were like a ship. Your course was set.

Sometimes erratic she veered, went off her set course.

Other ships moved in ever widening circles, in jungle darkness, aimlessly, by water surrounded, landless, seeking land. You held the wheel, dizzily clung on. He held on, holding Kay. You had to watch the currents, the whirl-pool.

"She didn't know what she wanted," Gaunt said, "didn't know when she was well off."

The tone of his voice was harsh, old grudges pregnant there.

"That's a weakness, not a vice," Father Michaels said. "The long holiday was the failure there, a doctor would have been more wise. You were in the wrong, perhaps."

"It was all a farce. She was false. I see that now."

He saw Kay now, saw her coming into the saloon of the *Aurora*, come towards him. He did not know how long he had been sitting at the table, alone. He remembered similar nights. He thought how dull and boring he must have been to her. He looked up from the table, saw her doll-like prettiness, she was admiring herself in the mirror. She was thirty-eight. He was fifty-one. The table was between them, a desert, the waste of years lay there, he could see it all. He still loved her in spite of the waste.

"We had a row that night," Gaunt said. "We were supposed to be going out to meet my son. I thought, 'Well, Denis will mend things, he'll be the link.' 'Well,' I said, 'only two more days now. Did you send the wire?'

"I was buoyed up, I thought, 'Thank God for that.' It began with a holiday because she wanted a change. The holiday lasted for ten years."

He thought of ten years of cruising, each year like a flag, blowing in the wind, a little tattered, "Kimberley" gone, the roots up, the old circle scattered, the spurts of restlessness that swept them on from place to place. He went right back to the beginning.

They had been happy once. He talked of "Kimberley," the home he had built, his concern in the city; he was doing well. There had been Julie, but she had died very young. It was a blow to them both, but they had got over it. He hadn't noticed any great change in her. They were very much in love with one another. So old landmarks came back to him, ghosts.

The nine-fifty to town was running again, Kay was waving to him at the gate. He picked up Staveley at Alton. He was his partner. They talked of the market, money, told a dirty story, hastily remembered from dinner the night before. He thought of daily lunch at Todds.

"We were ideally happy. I had a passion for collecting things."

"What things?"

"Pictures, odds and ends, *objets d'art*, you know –" Gaunt said.

He thought of these things now, his pride in them, the celebration of a new addition to the collection at "Kimberley", Staveley down for the week-end, Kay looking her best, making him jealous, tall talk and small talk, and finally to wind up, the whole history of the new vase he'd got, quite a miracle to get hold of it at all, during which history Kay lay back in her chair slightly bored, Staveley gently snoring in the chair. And then, suddenly remembering, after Staveley had retired.

"What did you do to-day, darling?"

The smile was forced, the enthusiasm false as she described all she had done "to-day".

The train was still running, but now it seemed to carry nothing but his faults, his little weaknesses.

"And what did your wife do when you were away?" Father Michaels said.

Gaunt was silent. It seemed to require a great effort to remember, its sheer triviality dragged.

"Oh, I don't know. Little things, mostly the same sort of things every day. She went out in the morning, she had her hair done, she had coffee in a café, she rang up friends, called on her doctor, she had fresh ideas about her health every day, she lunched with a friend. She went home.

"Friends rang her up, returning the compliment, somebody came to tea. A ride in the car, an appointment with the dentist, a plan to run up to town to see a fashion show, the latest film. Mostly the same things each day."

"And were you interested in the things she did, the little things?"

"Why yes, I suppose I was," Gaunt stammered.

He could see her tiny hands waving at him. "Tired of it all." Of what? Their life? At thirty-eight? Of security, of him?

The anchor sunk fast, moved, loosening, it might come up suddenly, the ship move off. "Kimberley" was stoutly built, yet he could feel it beginning to tremble beneath his feet.

"I decided that very night," he said, and suddenly he remembered a good deal that day, a cheque in his pocket, the surprise for Kay. "I made plans. I decided she wanted a change, something different from the annual visit to Bognor, Torquay. I decided that very night. Whilst we talked it over I could see how restless she was."

"And you went away then?" Father Michaels said. "What about the boy?"

"He was at school. I made plans for him. He was to come into my business. A bright lad. Kay agreed on it, too. But suddenly she had another idea. She wanted him to go to Canada, to my sister there. She wanted to take him away from the school. I didn't agree with that. It seemed absurd to make such a violent break in a boy's life. I said he was best left where he was, we would only be away three months at the most. I had my business to think of, I made every arrangement with my partner. It was all settled, except the boy."

"He went to Canada. That's what was bringing you out?"

"He went. She saw to that. I was suspicious. I wondered why she suddenly wanted him out of the way."

"'We can't leave him at the school if it closes, can we, and we can't drag him all over the place with us,' she said.

"'But we'll only be away a couple of months,' I said, 'why d'you want Denis out of the way all of a sudden like this?'

"She never explained why, nor did I pursue the reason for her strange attitude. She must have talked him into it. I didn't realize then that she hadn't the slightest intention of return-ing to 'Kimberley', once she was out of it. I saw my son. I talked it over with him. I explained that his mother was unwell, that she wanted a change, we were going away for a fairly long holiday. I tried to persuade him to go down and stay with my brother until the school should re-open. But she had already made up his mind for him, he wanted to go out to Canada. She was an impulsive woman, nothing would have made her alter her mind. Denis went away, we both saw him off, he appeared quite happy. But I was worried about Kay.

"'This holiday'll do you good,' I said.

"She said she was certain of that, she wanted to get away, anywhere, at once. I agreed on that. I was afraid for her. We left the very next day. She dismissed the servants, closed the house."

"And you never went back there?"

Gaunt shook his head. He could see "Kimberley" quite clear

in his mind now, a hand drawing a black veil over the house.

"No! From that moment her restlessness increased. A doubt came into my mind. I thought perhaps she was in love with somebody else. I thought it was a plan long formed in her mind, and I hated myself for beginning to doubt, for being the slightest bit suspicious of her motives. It was all too sudden. It was a whim, I told myself, a mood, a good holiday would heal everything. I even told myself that she would return to 'Kimberley' loving it all the more, my mind was full of plans. I thought of Denis at home with us, the new interest in her life. I remember the morning we left, the moment we were in the train for London. 'Oh, John!' she said. 'At last!'"

He thought of the struggle to build, to reach a haven, to surround oneself with security, to have it all swept from under one's feet by Kay. He had cast anchor, settled in the calm of the bay, always conscious of the noisy waters beyond the quietude. He had tried hard not to hear them, his mind had refused to accept them.

"She was free," Gaunt said.

The anchor was up, the ship free, already eager to be off towards greater seas. Not for Kay the calm lake. He thought one was safe in the lake. One was lost in the ocean. The world had always been an ocean to him.

No different to this at which he stared, across which cities and towns, hotels, cars, trains and ships were already reeling.

"Waste," his mind said, "waste."

"It was only the beginning," Gaunt said.

A figure was coming towards them. It stopped. It was Benton standing there.

"Better come for your ration, Gaunt," he said.

Father Michaels did not notice for some minutes that Gaunt had got up and left him. When he looked round the seat was empty. His mind was tired again, he remembered somebody talking about a woman named Kay. His aged eyes looked down the boat. He saw a man rowing, three others seated in the stern. He thought he saw a man taking off his boot. At that moment a man got up and came to him. It was Curtain. He carried the cigarette tin, containing a mixture of water and condensed milk, a biscuit in his other hand. He looked up as the man approached. Was he looking grim? When the sailor sat down he looked again. But if there was grimness on the bearded face it was gone now.

"Here's your ration, Father Michaels."

Curtain was glad to see that the old man looked a little better, his spirits had brightened up, perhaps it had been the talk with Gaunt. He had been watching the two of them for some time. Father Michaels was waking up, becoming more like himself. Thinking of these things, he also thought of the water lessening, of biscuits the old man could not eat.

"I could soak one of these biscuits, Father," Curtain said, "you could easily eat it then."

"They make me feel sick – besides – my – teeth," wearily.

"You'll have to eat," great earnestness behind the sailor's utterance.

"I'll have to eat?"

"Yes, if you don't –" Curtain replied.

He took the tin from the sailor, gulped once, slobbered a little, handed back the tin.

"All of it, please," Curtain said, "it'll be a long time before you get another ration. Six hours perhaps."

The priest looked up at him.

"Drink it all up," Curtain said. He was not smiling now, he was looking worried. The priest smiled.

"That man Gaunt, he started to tell me a story, something about his life –" the voice faded away to a whisper, "life, trivial lives," and then he took the tin from Curtain again, made a valiant effort, and the tin was handed back empty. He ignored the proffered biscuit.

"That poor man," the priest said, "I was thinking about him just now. What about him, Mr. Curtain? His mother, his wife – think of that."

"It was hard lines. He's gone now. Let's forget about it," Curtain said, seeing Crilley for a swift moment, the full weight of the body across the water keg, limp, incomprehensible, unexplainable.

"If it hadn't been for that bloody searchlight he would have been with us now."

He could not forget Crilley, his mate. The resolve to be done with it broke down, the core of resolution shook in him. He thought of himself passing down a street in which many people were walking. He passed by a man, he did not know him, he would never remember him again. Come and gone in a flash. Crilley was like that. Crilley was a sailor. They went out that way.

"That chap Benton's beginning to worry me a bit," said Curtain, suddenly cursing himself for having mentioned it.

Father Michaels was too old and too tired to be listening to anything about Benton.

"Benton?"

"You know, the young chap," his manner confiding, leaning against the priest, telling himself he didn't have much chance to talk to this old man. "His feet are troubling him. One's beginning to swell."

"If only the sun would come, the warm weather, everybody'd feel different at once."

The thin white hand went to the sailor's knee, shook there, pawed blindly at nothing. "I heard somebody say we were making for the traffic lanes. I didn't quite understand what was meant by that. Tell me, Mr. Curtain, was I very sick?"

"Very, very sick," Curtain said. "But everybody's been very sick. I was myself. It's nothing. Everybody's sick in a small boat."

"Sometimes I wish I could row. I would like to row."

Curtain looked away, thought, "By heck, I'd better shift him aft again." The look of things was not pleasant to him. The sun seemed worlds away.

"I think, Father Michaels, you could pray for us," he said, a big hand over that of the priest, patting it, again Father Michaels was the old baby, sitting up in its cot, wonder in its baby eyes.

"You oughtn't to sit up here all the time. You should come down, sit in with us. We often have talks together."

He wondered what Gaunt talked about; anything could upset an old man, who was now a little better, sipping some of the milk, who would be with them when the worst moments came, his eyes studying the changing waters, the light suddenly going, be with them when they got the warm weather, lay on their backs in the sun, drying clothes and bones.

Hearing a shout he got up and left the priest to his own company once more. He found Stone kneeling, Benton sitting

53

on a seat, clinging to it, Stone was endeavouring to get his boot off. Benton, making a mountain out of a molehill, protested. He didn't want the other boot off. It was only one foot that had swelled.

"Shut up, and less bloody gab out of you," Curtain growled, standing watching him, seeing one foot already swelled, seeing two feet that had stood a whole night in salt water, when Benton had been too sick to move. Now, he thought, he's making a damned row about nothing at all.

"After all, it's his bloody foot," he growled at Stone, winking. "give him his damn foot back again. I thought you were a good sailor, Benton. Crying about a little thing like your foot," seeing it full of bullets, Crilley in his mind, gone again in a flash.

"Stone, you'd better cut along there, do a spot of work with Gaunt."

When Stone had joined Gaunt at the oars, Curtain seized Benton by the shoulders, shook him angrily, said, "Blast you!"

"What's up?" Benton said, astonished, a little afraid, a new side of Curtain confronting him, looking more boyish than ever to the sailor.

"I'll tell you. You're a stupid young swine. Give me that foot, come on, give it here. I'm having no more bloody nonsense here. We've enough to worry about without your feet," and he grabbed Benton's foot, threw him off his balance. He began pulling at it. Picking at the wet laces he broke a finger nail, swore under his breath.

"You'd think you were dying, blast you."

He thought of how stupidly stubborn men could be, thinking of Father Michaels, refusing time after time to have his collar removed, "Probably choke him to death one of these nights." It was so bloody silly, besides making the atmosphere more uncomfortable. The others noticed every little thing. And Stone when he was sick. They irritated him.

"You shouldn't be lying down at all, only making it worse. You want your head in the fresh air all the time, not stuck in that mess of yours."

He remembered these little things, and the sulkiness of Gaunt. His stupid silence for a whole day and night. Again he wished Jennins or Grimes were with him. He began massaging Benton's foot.

"Oh hell, go easy, Curtain," Benton cried, giving a jump.

"I'm only trying to help you, damn you," Curtain shouted in his face.

"Why didn't you leave the bloody thing alone."

"Goddam your foot," shouted Curtain, and pushed Benton off the seat. His rage was sudden, blind, short-lived, the first rage since he had got into the boat with them.

"I have to rely on them. They on me." He joined Gaunt and Stone. He watched them, he had nothing to say to them. He just noticed how they rowed, that the sea was dark blue in colour, the sky a black curtain against this.

Long rowing had a hypnotic effect upon one. Sometimes he noticed it in Stone and Gaunt. He himself had been like it, too. One lulled oneself into a sort of trance-like state. If a sea came over, one could be washed away by this, lifted over the side, wafted away, resigned, helpless, there would be no bodily form of protest. It was a kind of surrender. But at night it was different. One watched then, was aware, darkness opened wider the eyes. Stone looked at Curtain, Curtain at them both. Stone saw Benton leaning over the stern as though he were watching for something in the water. He had heard him shout, saw him go over the seat. Nobody spoke. A silence that seemed final and complete came over the boat. For the first time the head of the old priest had ceased to bob. Curtain glanced his way. No longer was he the old sea-bird come home to roost on the bow of the boat. Curtain sat still.

From this silence he made walls, behind which he hid, he gave his thoughts free rein, forgot the men in front of him, forgot Benton's foot, the priest's collar. He wandered far away from them all. There were hours like this, forming barriers against one another, when doors in their minds shut down, their faces masks, themselves hidden behind them. A pressure was released, the invisible chain holding them together as men broke, scattered, they were free, locked in little worlds of their own.

Curtain thought of his home, his last trip, his bad luck, his next ship, he went down different streets of his life, recognizing old faces, voices, landmarks. He was seeing Jane, Nell pulling on his hand whilst he told her of Crilley. "Poor old Jack."

The air was alive with a word. "Ship! Ship!" Benton cried.

All oars dragged water, arms waved frantically, lips moved, "Ship! Ship!"

The three men jumped to their feet, Father Michaels struggled to get up, staggered, fell back in his seat.

"God!" Gaunt said. "A ship!"

The word sprung like a claw, swift upon withering hope. The three men clung to each other, arm gripping arm, whilst Benton, wild, shouting, cried, "Ship! Ship!"

Curtain broke loose and ran down to him. "Where is this ship, Benton?"

"There!" Benton shouted, "Hell, wave something, wave

something," and Gaunt came running up, "Yes, wave some-thing, my God, wave something," and his coat was off, flying about his head, the pupils of his eyes dilated.

"I can't see, I can't see. Where is this bloody ship?"

"Where?" Curtain said, hoping and not hoping, doubting, hands to his eyes, staring out.

"There!" Benton said, shaking the other's arm, then pointing, stretching his body up, so that he overbalanced, and would have been over the side but that Stone flung out a hand and caught him, pulled him back.

"You mean there? A point to starboard, there?" Curtain said, algebra to Benton, who screamed, "Bloody hell, are you blind, can't you see?" forgetting the ship, thinking of his swollen foot, Curtain pulling on it a little while ago.

Hands went to eyes, Stone ransacking the skyline, Gaunt waving like one mad, the priest in a squeaky voice crying out, "Help me up, up – help –"

"Goddam, I can't see anything," Curtain said, low in his throat, "are you quite sure, Benton, you see –"

"My God!" Stone shouted, "we may have missed it, we may have missed it, missed the ship – ship," hands falling to his sides, helpless, hope hollow, no longer believing, scowling at Curtain whose back was to him.

"Where the hell was the thing when you saw it?"

"I told you. *There!*" the words spiked, ready to wound Curtain, who was "blind", too calm for him. "There," Benton said again, still pointing, shouting in Gaunt's ear, "Wave, wave."

So their voices rose, sped out on wings of hope, circled ocean and came back to them. Curtain's body moved slowly, his eyes scanning every square inch of ocean, his mind tortured by doubt, searching for the tell-tale wisp of smoke, the shadow, the substance of the object that moved, that would speak to them of eyes watching over seas, eyes that Gaunt and Stone remembered now, "You are never really lost, somewhere there are eyes watching out for you. The seas had lanes like cities and towns. Somewhere there was a ship. You had to keep cool, hold on," echoes of Curtain's words buzzing in their ears like bees.

"Perhaps you saw it abeam. Where in the name of hell are you pointing to? Heaven!" Curtain shouted in Benton's face, shouting to cover the confusion in his mind, the thought of no ship there, an illusion, of their faces facing him, mirrors of their nerves.

"It's there! I can see it now," Benton cried out, ran forward waving, towards the priest, who looked at him wide-eyed, open mouthed, wondering, seeing the other three rush after him.

"For God's sake," Curtain said, his mind crying for calm, "for God's sake sit down. Will you, please?" his hands on Benton's shoulders, pressing him down, down.

"And you, Gaunt, sit down. Stone, too. Listen to me. I wouldn't blame this kid if he imagined he saw a ship, it's nothing, other men have seen ships before him. You get excited, you reach past yourself, you think you've missed the ship, the bloody sea expands, drives you crazy looking at it. I know. Just sit still and keep cool. I'll talk to Benton when I'm satisfied about this ship."

He stood, back to them, peering out towards the skyline, eyes straining beyond this, behind patches of cloud, he could miss nothing who had watched from decks, and from the heights above them, not once, but many times. He turned then, and Benton was crying. It touched Curtain. He felt sorry for him, understanding him, saying in his mind, "If only it had been a ship."

"Sometimes when one is looking out on water like that, moving water, and the sky so still against it, you fancy things, things are moving there, you think, sometimes you see smoke. I understand. Better luck next time, Benton. Isn't that so, Stone, you there, Gaunt, isn't that so? You imagine things sometimes, torment yourself for hours afterwards, believing the ship *was* a ship after all, and now it's gone by," looking at Stone and Gaunt, his eyes saying, "This is only a bit of a kid, he's crying, that will do him good."

He began patting Benton on the shoulder, his eyes on the old priest who had not uttered a word, whilst the other two looked out to sea, gave the last tug at hope, whole fleets of ships sailing across their minds.

"This bloody water," Benton cried.

"Easy there, son," Curtain said.

"Going round in circles, where are we going, where?"

"Control yourself. What did I tell you about walking on that foot of yours. Remember what I said to you that first morning? Have you forgotten? Suppose your girl in Somerset saw you now," his voice soft, hand on Benton's hair, Gaunt and Stone still staring out, their backs to him, staring, staring. Suddenly they walked away, went to their places amidships, but they let the oars drag water, not caring much, not hoping much, doubting. The light was going, the afternoon wearing down. They talked in whispers, doubting Curtain. He had been the signal in their minds, this was down. The language of the ocean was alien to them, Curtain had the key to this. They wondered about him now.

59

"You see," Stone said, "we have to rely on him absolutely. This man says we have rowed nearly eighty miles, perhaps a hundred, how do we know? But who can count miles in this?" arms circling, embracing the seas. "He says he is making for the traffic lanes, ships will be about there. He says we will be picked up soon. Two days now, nearly three, is it three or four, he says the sun will come, we will get dried, warm, everything will be all right. We have to believe him. How do we know? Suppose Benton did see a ship, suppose –" a flood of words came, on the crest of desperation's surge, tiredness of this wilderness, a mumble of sounds from dry lips, incoherent to Gaunt.

"I don't know," Gaunt said, "my mind drifts like the boat, I don't care much, you see –" he stopped suddenly, his eyes avoided those of Stone, who doubted Curtain now, and once he had believed in him, faithful, trusting.

"He lost contact with those boats," Gaunt said, "he said the wireless was smashed, he said lots of things. I remember them."

"He says the water is going down," Stone said, his mind searching for faults, flaws in the wheel, tripping Curtain up, remembering him being angry with Benton, "a mere kid," he said, "he asks us to stand by him, and we stand by, three days in this boat, how many damn hours is that, even the old man up there is weary of it all, just look at him. He says nothing, but he thinks a lot. Why shouldn't Benton see a ship? His eyes are no different to that sailor's eyes."

"If we drown, he'll drown too," Gaunt said. His lips were dry, he wondered when rations would be issued again, he did not want any more biscuit, only water, water.

"I told him the other night; I said, 'You can't do that. You can't bury that man like that, and a priest there.'"

"What man?"

"That sailor Crilley who was killed," Stone said, "he pushed him over, I saw him do it. He said he could do it quite easily, he said he knew his prayers as well as any priest, he said –"

Complaints piled, grumbles gathered speed, suspicion stirred. So these encircled Curtain.

V

THE WORLD REELED, AND Curtain watched it reel. The oars were in, the sea anchor held, she was hove to, the boat wild, threshing water coming in as fast as he baled it out. Darkness had come, stars dancing in the sky. He was sat there in the darkness, his eyes watched for each down-rushing sea. Sky met water, water leaped to sky. He sat alone. He had expected this, had seen it coming. The movements of clouds were as words to him, a language he could understand. He had endeavoured to shift the old priest aft, but he could not move him. He was too ill for that. The old man was lying with his head on the seat, and he did not hear the sailor when he spoke to him, nor open his eyes.

"You can't stay here," Curtain said, bending down, two arms round the priest, "you can't stay here," thinking how this old man was worth all the rest of them put together, slowly lifting him up.

"Oh, please – let me go, let me go," eyes still closed, whilst Curtain held him in mid-air.

"But we're slipping water, you'll be drowned," he said, not caring about the others now, only this old man, God's innocent lost. The priest groaned, begged.

"Put me down, put me down."

He had put him down, but first he had to put him further back, making him comfortable in the boat bottom, going clumsily forward in the darkness, hands groping, finding the spare canvas, the sacking with which to make him comfortable for the night. There had been no ration for him, he could not drink or eat. It made Curtain sad looking at him, who had seemed so well in the early morning, touching his forehead, feeling it hot and clammy. He was afraid, not of the boat being swamped, only of fever coming to this man, old, fragile, who had not complained, who had even wanted to row, making him laugh, who had been so quiet, cheery, smiling, trying to smile, vomiting, helpless. Afraid only of his dying who had been slowly recovering, who had sat there listening to a man named Gaunt, talking "about some bitch name of Kay".

Curtain could not break down the stubbornness in Benton's mind, the ship was still there, he had seen it, he was sure of that. He could not speak to Gaunt, who had helped him with the sea anchor before darkness was finally upon them. He could not do this because Gaunt himself was silent. Curtain had wondered why, why Gaunt had looked at him in the old way, when first he had inquired his name. He could not speak with Stone, who had talked about him to Benton, mistrusting him; he had heard them both, heard Stone lighting up the ship in Benton's mind. So it seemed to him this distrust was growing and he was afraid of that. One could not row up mountains, so he had hove to, told them to draw in their oars. The sea had been mountains in the darkness. They had drawn them in, in silence, wondering at this. Soon it was full dark.

Slowly it had dawned on the sailor how they were whispering to each other about him, whose ear and eye were poised, watching ahead, listening. A head wind was driving down, carrying with it great arcs of whirling spray, the boat's nose went down, reared and plunged again.

He had expected this. Not a ship, not a bird, nor sight of anything save this reeling world. He was sat there a minute or so, then Gaunt, he thought it was Gaunt, not seeing clearly, got up and went away. And later another got up, he knew it was Stone. They had left him without a word, carrying doubt with them, shadow grown to substance, frayed nerves, and he was sad at this.

He sat there, his body slumped, hands clasped, letting his body be one with the boat, and water was coming in. He had set to work, forgetting, ignoring them, bent down for hours, baling water.

Somewhere they were sitting or lying, holding tight to them this sudden doubt.

"Good God!" he said.

"Only three days. I thought they could come through without their nerves giving way, it's that silly little bastard of a kid, Benton," astonishment flashing through his mind like light. "I thought things were getting better, their sicknesses over. I got them together, I talked to them. I said everything will be all right so long as you keep your heads. I'll get you out of this."

He repeated this in his mind, slowly, laboriously his mind climbing a hill, repeated all he had said to them, as he watched the seas, sky reel, clouds hover. And then he stood up, his back aching, ice in his bones, his body crying sleep. Why had they believed in Benton and not him? It was this fellow Gaunt, queer in his head, gabbling in an old man's ear, "Some bitch name of Kay".

Gaunt was the sea swamping them, the ache in his back, the sudden feeling of uncertainty. When Gaunt wasn't rowing he was sleeping, or sitting for'ard talking to the priest.

"Perhaps there's something in him that the old man likes," he reflected, "but he's hardly spoken three words to me since he came into this bloody boat. I have no grudge against the fellow."

Once he had been standing near when Gaunt and the priest were talking. Something about his wife who had led him on, how he had been a fool, she had never really loved him, had been in love with another man for years. How he had been blind to it, how she had even followed this man from place to place, dragging Gaunt after her, money wasted like water. How she had lied to him even on the last night aboard the *Aurora*. No wire had gone to the son. Tricked to the hilt.

He recalled the old priest talking to Gaunt.

"Your fault, Gaunt. You were a weak creature, you had no will."

He remembered saying to Stone, "She must have been a thorough bitch," how Stone had laughed.

"She didn't have enough to do, and he would always have made silly mistakes," Stone said.

Hitting the nail on the head.

Yet he felt sorry for the man, who, weak or not, had loved his wife. And now he didn't know whether she was alive or dead. Nothing for him to go back to, the son a stranger.

"It's all being emptied out on the poor old priest," Stone said.

These things came into Curtain's mind as he stood there with the baler in his hand. He could not see Gaunt now, but he knew where he was. Flat on his back, and so was Benton. A figure came up to him. It was Stone. The man was groping for, finally seized his hand.

"My bloody nerves," he said, "I'm sorry about this."

"Forget it," Curtain said. "Get aft there and search about for a baler like this," holding it close for the man to see, "then come back here and give a hand, unless you want to drown. Gaunt and the other fellow can stay put, they'll be more use to us sleeping, believe me. A pair of bloody nuisances. If they slept three days running it might save the water," laughing. "It's going down."

"Going down," Stone exclaimed, "going down?"

"Yes, down. Don't expect it'll last for ever, do you?"

"I suppose –"

"Christ! Don't stand there supposing," he shouted in Stone's face.

He was on his knees again, baling, when Stone returned and joined him. He started in furiously, once their heads met, once their balers crashed together, but no word was spoken. Stone was definitely worried. He felt a little ashamed, he told himself he had been carried away by Benton, had mistrusted Curtain, who, from the beginning had relied on him.

"You're not really mad with me, are you?" he said, squatting on his heels.

Curtain dropped his baler.

"Why should I be mad with you, with anybody except a man who takes water from the keg when nobody is looking."

"Who?"

"Gaunt," Curtain said. "I said nothing about it, I won't either. He'll get half a tinful of water for his next ration. I'm not mad with you, why the hell should I be? These things happen, I've seen it all before. This morning I heard you saying to Benton that Gaunt was suffering in his mind. Perhaps he is, but others may suffer if he pinches any more water. That's all. You just got to hope for the best, not lose your bloody nerve."

"Curtain," said Stone, "tell me this. D'you really think we'll be found? I can't help asking that. The way you go about, the things you say, the things you do, I say to myself, 'That man is cool. He must be sure.'"

"Don't you believe it for a moment. I'm no more sure than you are. I'm hopeful, because all I've seen in my lifetime makes me feel like that," he concluded, and a silence fell between them, broken only by the sound of the balers scraping boat bottom, the curious sound water made as it was scooped into them. He looked up suddenly at Stone. "Benton's useless. His other foot is beginning to swell. If only we got the sun –"

"Yes," Stone said, worlds away, "yes," not thinking of Benton but of the water stolen by Gaunt, Curtain's remarks in his mind.

Sometimes Stone glanced over Curtain's head at the great sheets of cloud that passed over and obscured the patches of sea, so that it appeared as though an early morning haze were riding over the waters. Once there seemed no light at all, and the boat was bobbing about on the edge of the world. He did not know how long he had been bent like this, his arm moving to and fro like a pendulum. Something told him that he must keep at it, he dare not stop while Curtain's own arm rose and fell. He wondered then why Gaunt did not come along and help. Benton was useless, hardly able to walk now, but Gaunt was all right. He wondered if he should mention this to Curtain. And he did.

"He's no damned use to me," argued Curtain. "If I wanted Gaunt I wouldn't have asked you. Gaunt keeps the priest company. That's all I want him to do, for the present. And leave the bloody water alone, of course."

"Suppose we're never picked up," Stone ventured to say.

Curtain laughed. "We'd drown. For Christ's sake give us a rest."

Later he took the baler from Stone. "Clear out," he said, "clear out."

Stone allowed Curtain to take the baler from him, then he rose to his feet and walked away. He wanted to stay, he hesitated, but Curtain pushed him off, "Go ahead! Clear out."

He did not go, sinking down on to the seat. He slept where he sat.

He felt something warm upon his face, as though someone were breathing on him, and when he opened his eyes it was the sun, high in the sky, and the light streaming down. The great area of water was ablaze. He did not remember falling asleep, nor how long he had remained stretched on the seat, perhaps Curtain himself had laid him there, and then he saw that his feet had been secured to the seat by a length of rope. Curtain had tied him. A high sea had been running, he remembered that, and the strong head wind sending seas down on their little boat. Half the night he had helped Curtain to keep the boat from being swamped, they had knelt opposite each other, but they had not spoken much. Curtain had been silent, he recalled that, rather sullenly so. This had worried him. Slowly he sat up and looked about him. He saw Benton and Gaunt at the oars. They conversed in excited whispers with each other.

"Wonder what's happened," Stone asked himself.

As suddenly he forgot them, lay on his back again, staring upwards, a sky of the clearest blue. He sat up again, slowly he undressed. Naked, he lay along the seat, lay quite still. Not thinking only feeling the warmth pass into his body, lying there with closed eyes, mind vacant, warmth melting all thought away. He lay motionless, like a fish. Warmth touched his bones, his blood began to tingle, he exulted in the sunshine. Words and the echoes of words floated by him, were flooding his ears. He heard nothing save a buzzing sound. He had scattered his clothes to dry. Half sitting again he saw Curtain right for'ard, bent over the priest. And the sailor's eye saw Stone, a glance at a too familiar object, he forgot him; Stone might have been a dead fish.

Father Michaels was stretched out on a seat, and he was naked. Curtain was massaging him. Near by his clothes hung on a line to dry.

As he endeavoured to get some life into the body of the priest, he was curiously unmindful of the sun. He hardly noticed it, never looked up, just went quietly on, rubbing the man's body. He felt a sense of triumph at getting the old priest's clothes off. In the night he had been taken ill again.

Curtain had found him shivering. Now he suddenly shouted down the boat. "Stone! Where the hell are you?"

Naked, Stone picked his way to Curtain.

"You'd best bring your clothes along here," Curtain said. "Sit by the old man here, but don't bother him with talk. He's too sick for that. Just keep your eye on him, if anything goes wrong, shout me."

He went and stood over the two men at the oars. He told Benton to stand up. He tried to do so but fell down again.

"And that's another," thought Curtain, lifting Benton out of his seat; the oars dragged water; he carried Benton aft.

"You're so damn stubborn," said Curtain, "that other boot's coming off."

He started to undo the boot, and Benton winced. "Shut up," he said.

The boot came off, feeling like pulp in the sailor's hand.

"This feller's useless, too. I thought he could stand it. Anyhow, he can't."

"You must have them rubbed, you don't want them getting bloody worse, do you?"

"I don't care what happens to them," Benton said.

"But I do," Curtain said, rubbing at the foot, almost lost to sight between his two hands.

"There's Stone," he thought, "and he's all. Well, one is better than none," and from time to time he shot glances at Gaunt.

To-morrow he'd be down. "A lovely crew," fiercely, under his breath. "You can make yourself comfortable. Lie there, that's all you have to do. Make the best of it."

The sun was shining, but there was no time to see the sun. He returned to the old man. "How does he look to you, Stone?"

"Not too bad, he could be worse."

"As soon as you're through you'd best take over from Gaunt. No need to look twice at him. You got to stand by me, Stone. These others –" not looking at the man, but watching the priest, eyes closed, skin wax-like, a thin and transparent face under the light.

Father Michaels opened his eyes. "Give me a drink," he said. He looked beyond Curtain, beyond Stone, at anything, at nothing. "Give me a drink," he said.

"You can give out the rations," Curtain said, "half a tinful to each man, one biscuit."

"You're not very ill, you know," he said, bending over the priest, "you'll be all right in a tick. See, look up, there's the sun. It's sitting in those damp clothes," and then the priest opened his eyes, and Curtain was shaking a finger in his face. "You should've let me take those clothes off long ago."

Stone came back. He poured water into the old man's mouth.

"Now you'll feel better," Curtain said, "soon's your things are dry you can have them back again."

"I've given Benton his," Stone said, "he threw away the biscuit."

"You picked it up?"

"No! I came with this water for him," pointing to the old man.

"Go and pick the biscuit up," Curtain said, taking the tin from Stone.

Gaunt's eyes opened wider as he saw the water being issued out, he became unduly excited, the hands on the oars made little convulsive movements, he dropped the oars, waiting.

"That's yours," Curtain said, handing the tin to Gaunt.

"Is that all?"

"Afraid so."

"My God, is that all there is?" the tin shaking in his hand.

"Yes, and don't spill what you've got, either. We want some for to-morrow."

He gulped the water, choking, spluttered, "Where the hell are we going?"

"Early this morning I saw you messing about aft. Did you take some water out of the keg?" asked Curtain.

"Yes. A drop."

"All right! I'll say nothing this time, except that you may have taken another man's share. Don't do it again." He looked at Gaunt, all the weaknesses in him seemed to flood the features.

"We're all damn sorry about your wife," Curtain said, "but we have other things to think about besides that. I thought I'd have a little chat with you. You haven't been very talkative. I know why. You haven't been very civil either, to anybody here, and that I just couldn't understand, because all of us here are men like yourself. You don't look like a person who could stand much. The priest can stand less, and he was taken real ill last night. So d'you mind if I ask you to keep away

71

from him for a bit, instead of talking all the time?"

"Where the hell are we going? How long are we going to be like this?"

"I can't tell you. I wish I could. I told you all that first day, didn't I? Nice bloody way you respond. Benton's flat on his back. No use to me. There's Stone and yourself. Three of us, we'll get some place in time," rising slowly to his feet, "but if you go stealing water you might find your position changed. I mightn't care, Stone mightn't –"

"I thought you said we were making for –"

"We are."

Curtain sat down again. "You should try and cheer up, if only for appearance sake. There's an old man with us, and an excitable youngster, there's Stone. Benton has a girl, Stone has a family, so have I. That's why we're pulling ahead. Benton says we're going round in circles, but who minds what a lad says? The priest says nothing, except his prayers. We have to stand by one another, Gaunt. Just an hour ago I had a row with Stone, it couldn't be helped, we rely on each other."

"I don't know what the hell's wrong with me – I don't know –" Gaunt said, hands fumbling, pulling at Curtain.

Curtain was touched by this, he thought the man was going to cry, and then he cried, and he could not remember ever seeing a man cry.

"No need to worry about anything, your life as well as ours. Now you've been rowing a good while, go and have a lie down. Go and have a chat with the kid there. You have to keep your mind off that experience you had, it's getting you down. Cheer up, for heaven's sake, we're not lost. Only three days in the bloody boat, suppose we were a whole week – I'd begin to get worried myself."

He was patting the man on the back, he was thinking of Benton's feet, he was watching the priest, he was wondering how long Stone would stick it.

"Go long aft and make yourself comfortable," and he pushed Gaunt away, sat down in his place and took his oars.

"If only he'd sit here with us and talk a bit, instead of thinking about that bitch of a woman he had; she must have been a bitch considering what I heard. A shock, but we all get bloody shocks. Wants taking out of himself, mind's too much on one thing."

He thought of Gaunt spilling his life story into the ears of an old priest, who half the time could not have heard him, remembered taking water to Father Michaels one afternoon, and Gaunt getting up immediately, going off like a kid who's been caught pinching from the larder, shy, awkward, not like a man, and his saying, "I don't know what you've been gassing about, but he hasn't heard a word you've said. He's fast asleep." A gaunt, thin man. How well the name suited him.

"Seems to have had money to burn, too," reflected Curtain. He supposed if they got back safe this man would build up another business, forget his experience, build up his life again. He had seen many people like Gaunt, they travelled about the world, never settling in any particular place, just moving about. It seemed odd to him, who had a wife and family, and they had been living in the one house for twenty-two years. Sometimes his sympathy was vague, undetermined, his mind could swing to the opposite extreme, and he could say, "Serves him right, a pair of bloody rotters they must have been." The two poles of right and wrong stood erect in his mind, no flags, no decorations flew from them. He could be sorry for Gaunt, he could loathe him, and he could be patient with him, too.

VI

"THERE!" STONE SAID, "now you'll be all right," and he stood
back to look at Father Michaels, as though he had been dressing
a doll, a pride welling up in him at a feat accomplished. The
old man was all bones, it had been quite a job. But it was done
now, and there he was, nice and comfortable in his old place,
his back against the seat, head resting on the folded coat. Stone
had forgotten he himself was naked, he might never have
worn clothes. "You feel better now," he said.

The priest made an effort, smiled. "You're Stone, aren't you."

Stone sat closer. "I'm Stone," he said.

"You think this man Curtain will get us through?" after a fit
of coughing.

"As certain of that as I am of my name."

"I keep looking out for a ship but I never see anything," the
priest said.

"Curtain will see one before we do. Let me fix that coat,"
seeing it slip from beneath the priest's head.

"Suppose we never see a ship again. I've been wondering
about that. I wonder if that woman is alive. I wonder if the other
boats are safe now. I think we're lost, and Mr. Curtain is afraid
to say so."

"How beautiful the sea looks now," Stone said, "and yet how lonely it is," changing the subject.

"Is that Gaunt over there?" Father Michaels said.

"Yes, and there's Benton, too. He can't walk very well, his feet are badly swollen," he whispered in the old man's ear, "they had a row, Benton and Curtain. The sailor chap thinks Benton's a little light in the head," tapping his own head.

Father Michaels became alert, he sat up suddenly, throwing off his lassitude, he stared down at Curtain. "He said that?"

"Yes," Stone said, and realized what he had done. Broken his promise to Curtain. "Listen, you won't say a word about this, will you?" hand on the priest's hand.

"No, No! I won't say a word. But fancy that. Poor fellow. He's hardly spoken to me," and after a pause, "how helpless we all are, how helpless," and then he was tired again, the eyes closed and opened like shutters, making Stone think of a cat sitting in front of a warm fire. He left him then, went aft to get his clothes.

"Asleep?" asked Curtain as Stone passed him by.

"Yes. He half looks at you, half listens, his mind must be continually dazed," thinking, "he won't remember what I said about Benton." He began to dress, watching Benton and Gaunt as he did so. He saw Gaunt watching him through half-closed eyes, he thought his face had grown much thinner in the past three days. Benton's swollen feet were resting on the seat, head and body lay in the bottom of the boat. Something comical about his attitude made Stone laugh. Like an answer to this Gaunt laughed, but he did not look at him. And then Benton was laughing, too. They all laughed, the boat seemed to shake under it. Curtain, looking up from the oars seemed not surprised, nobody had laughed here since he could remember.

75

He had expected this. It was the sun, the warmth, the light. They flashed out of his mind again, and he forgot the odd look on Benton's face. Stone, now dressed, came and sat by him. They rowed together.

"I was thinking about that last place Gaunt and his wife were," Curtain said suddenly. "I can't pronounce the name. It must be bloody dull for Gaunt here, mustn't it? Same faces, same sea. It's got him down, the silence. That's what's wrong with the kid. The Thames wasn't big enough when he rowed on it." He spat over the side.

"Oh! That was a place in France," Stone said. "Cannes, in the south. Were you ever in an open boat before?"

"I was. We were all sailors though. Ten days a long while ago, that."

"That was bad," Stone said.

"While it lasted. You get over things. Look at the old priest. Must be seventy to a day, why he'll be as lively as a cricket as soon as he steps out of this boat."

Heavy, lumbering thoughts in Stone's mind were suddenly lightened, bright colours flying there, as he listened to Curtain talking.

"Give him a few days' rest and he'll never remember being in this boat," Curtain continued. "You'll be the same, you couldn't be any different. It's only lousy while it lasts. The kid's different. He just won't come up to scratch."

Stone was not listening now, he was looking out over the water.

"Beautiful, isn't it?" he said.

"And deep."

Curtain laughed. Talking for the sake of talking, "And better than launching ships on it that are no bloody use to any man," he thought, seeing Benton's imagined ship stem to stern. That was the danger. Kidding yourself up. Thinking the world was just beyond the horizon line, thinking the ocean was flat and solid, and "beautiful", you read about it sometimes, "But it's just wet to me."

"Talking for the sake of talking," he said in his mind. "I wish the other two would talk for the sake of talking."

"You know, I was thinking just now how odd it was that Gaunt missed his wife, if as he says he actually saw her, but couldn't reach her. Now how the hell could a man miss his wife? A queer yarn altogether. He might have wanted to get rid of her, you never know."

"He wanted to get rid of her, no, she wanted to get shut of him," Stone said.

They skirmished with their subjects, talked of the most trivial things, surrounded Gaunt with a mass of theories, put Benton back in Somerset, gave Father Michaels a new collar and helped him into his church.

"Talking for the sake of talking," thought Curtain. Somewhere deep down in him, Mum and Nell stood, they were secure there, they could not be moved.

"I suppose you'll have to settle back again into your old job," said Curtain, suddenly pulling up a sleeve of Stone's shirt, "You're getting muscles."

Stone laughed. "Yes, a regular Samson. No, when I get back I'll have a rest, then take another boat out."

"Hope you have better luck then. By the way, can you swim, Stone?"

Stone sat up at that. "What?" he said.

"Swim?"

"Yes, why?"

"Nothing, just wondered."

You had to talk about something, you had to wear the hours down, the grinding, futile hours. You had to make pictures and fill your mind with them, you had to shut the ocean out. You knew they were worried, sometimes scared stiff, tormenting themselves, tossing about in their sleep, you had to pretend they weren't worried, that you knew them, that you knew them right down to the nerve centre, when you didn't really know them at all. You had to look at them and believe in them. You did this to keep balance. Coolness, control, these were ballast in your boat, her even keel, the power in the hand, behind each stroke of the oar.

Above their heads the sky stood still, the blaze of fire flung out rays, downpouring, fanwise upon their heads.

"I told them we'd run into the warm weather, but they wouldn't believe me," Curtain said.

"How long will it last?"

It was something too good to believe. "Perhaps we may sight something before nightfall," Stone said, a long, hopeful sigh in his voice, that suddenly broke under the words that Curtain spoke.

"Which reminds me," Curtain said, "you'd better bring that water down here. From now on I'm going to sleep on it. It may get warmer, who knows, we shall want all our water. I take no chances. Best go and do that right away."

Stone went, passed Benton and Gaunt, the positions of their bodies had not changed.

"You ought to dry those clothes, Gaunt," he said, so holding back words Gaunt himself was on the point of uttering. "I say, you ought to dry those clothes while you have the chance. You too, Benton."

No answer.

He picked up the keg, put it on his shoulder, they watched him do this, said nothing. Stone went off with it, put it under the seat where Curtain sat. Gaunt and Benton continued their whisperings.

"That's right. Stick it down there," said Curtain. "As from to-morrow a third of a tin full for each man, biscuit optional."

"How long will this really last, Curtain?"

"How the hell can I tell you that?"

"What about that milk then?"

"That's the priest's milk. Nobody else's."

"Oh – I see –" Stone replied, dreamily, not understanding the simple statement incomprehensible.

"I know what it is," he said to himself, "I'm dry – dry."

"When's the next ration? Christ, there's no time or anything here."

"You're thirsty, I know. So am I. We all are. But we must stay thirsty. I'm sorry, Stone, that's the position. Think of Gaunt pinching it from the keg. I could have killed him. Think of his mouth to the hole, spilling it. You have to have patience. I may have to knock you down, Stone," smiling at him, then feeling the dryness of his own lips, cursing Gaunt, laughing in the man's face, "but you're like me, you can keep cool, keep a hold on yourself. That will bring us through."

Talking for the sake of talking. Benton and Gaunt talked too.

"It might easily have been a ship that time," Gaunt said. "Suppose we are going round in circles?"

"Well?"

"Everybody'll go mad; my God, each time I think of it."

"What! What! Think of what?"

"Hell, I don't know," Gaunt said, licking his lips.

79

"Stone's taken the water away," Benton said. "I wonder why he did that?"

"They'll have a drink together when we're not looking," Gaunt said, a sickly smile then, followed by a burst of laughter, "your feet feel like balloons I suppose."

"You don't think for a moment he's lying to us?"

"How the hell do I know?" a whole river of lies in spate, surging down, Kay tossing in the middle of them.

"Suppose we are found, saved, I mean," Gaunt continued, "you'll go back to your girl, marry her?"

"I might, I don't know," cautiously, "what the devil d'you mean?"

"Nothing. I had a home once, a lovely home, then my wife got restless as hell and wasn't satisfied until she'd seen everything except the Taj Mahal; I was broke by that time. She may have got in the boat, she may not, I don't know. She used to say I was selfish, I wish I had been. I wouldn't be here now. She tore her way through everything I ever built up, and lied down to the last minute."

"Why?" Benton asked, watching Gaunt's eyes, his tongue on his lips, he began licking them again, he suddenly licked his own.

"I don't know. Didn't know when she was well off. Wanted the bloody moon. She's gone, and my son's gone, too. She told him a pack of lies –"

"But what for? There must have been some reason –" the words were like salt on the other's lips.

"Christ, don't keep on asking me questions," Gaunt said, "I don't know. I DON'T KNOW. I wasn't talking about that, anyhow," and he stopped suddenly, his mouth closed like a door, he was the spring of a clock run down.

He leaned against Benton. "That old priest was the only one who would listen to me," a hand on Benton's foot, stroking it, "your foot's swollen worse since Curtain removed the boot, some people know everything."

"My girl'll get a shock when she sees me; she won't expect me, that's the bloody fun of it," giggling. "I might catch her on the hop," a slow, dirty grin on his fleshy face. He began laughing.

"That priest will die, you can tell, just looking at him," Gaunt said, stroking Benton's other foot, "the way he breathes, and his eyes are glazed, he might be dead sometimes. I wonder if we'll see anything before it gets dark –"

"I wonder," Benton's eyes said, wide, feverish-looking, mouth open. "We've been three weeks in this infernal boat."

"They're quiet up there. Look at them. Listening to us all the time. Even stopped rowing to listen. They listen to everything. They work together. I heard them talking this morning about that priest. He won't last."

"You let the ship GO," Benton shouted into empty air. He fell back, his feet followed, he lay in a heap. Curtain watched all this.

"It's the silence. Just the silence of everything," speaking to Stone. "They've just had their rations. But it's the bloody silence of everything. I know. He'll be all right in a minute. They rave and toss, mostly scared, you can't do anything except let them tire themselves out. A mere kid. Should have stayed on the bloody Thames."

His hands gripped Stone's hands. "We stand together," he said, "we watch that, but we don't get worked up about it. Everything's terrible once, but not more than once. I mean sitting in this boat like this, waiting, watching, wondering.

You may be in another boat a year from now, but it's never the same."

"I understand," Stone said, was silent, but his eyes said, "I'm thirsty – thir – STY."

"So am I," thought Curtain. "I wish Jennins or Grimes were here. Poor Crilley. I hate seeing his missus, I hate it," and the thought spread, covered his mind, he forgot his dry lips, he was not thirsty thinking of Crilley. His tongue explored his mouth, he wanted to spit, spittle on the tip of it, he ran it round his mouth.

"How calm it is," Stone said, "yes, I see now. The silence."

"Best talk, even rot, anything, it helps," Curtain said, "and yet I'm surprised, we're not all that time in the boat, it might have been worse, still – remember that and you'll sleep to-night."

"You didn't sleep last night," Stone said, "I know."

"I can row," Curtain said, "and I can think of nothing. When I do that I'm not tired. Last night I thought more than once that everybody might have to bloody well swim for it, but it turned out O.K. When I saw the light coming, I saw the seas die down, and then the wind dropped, and I said to myself, 'Now we'll be safe, now the sun will come, I know, I knew it. It came just like that,'" and he flicked his finger and thumb, "and then I lay across those seats there and I fell asleep. I was sure."

"You tied me to the seat."

"As soon as you fell asleep. If you'd rolled off nobody would have noticed," smiling, "it would have been sad for you."

There seemed little of Curtain's face now, it was gradually disappearing behind a forest of hair.

"How did you get that stuff on your hair?"

Curtain's hand went to his head, he scratched vigorously.

"Don't know. Given up trying to find out, and I can't get the damned stuff off either," the other hand now helping with the scratching. He didn't feel itchy, mere mention of oil in it set him scratching. It was something to do, like picking your nails, or sending your dry tongue circling round your mouth, poking your ear.

Suddenly he said, "Listen! There's an old sound I know well. Stone you'd best go up there and see if all is well with the old chap. Take him a drop of milk in the tin."

When Stone pulled in his oars he knew how tired he was. "How long have we been rowing?" he asked.

"I don't know, I wasn't counting," Curtain said.

When Stone brought the tin along Curtain stirred the contents with the blade of his knife.

"He'll say he doesn't want it, which means he does. Just give it to him. Stay a while with him. Anything's better than Gaunt telling his life story. I'm sure the old man's too sick to be listening to that sort of stuff. Funny he should pick on him."

"We wouldn't be interested, I suppose," said Stone.

"He could be normal like any of us, he could come down here, sit with us, talk away if he liked; I think he likes being bloody queer." Stone went for'ard with the tin and sat down by the priest, who did not appear to notice his arrival. His profile stood out clearly against the light. Stone noticed the curious tensity, as though something in the old man strained for release. He put the tin down between his feet and sat back studying him. He wondered what he stared at with such rapt attention, "I wonder what he's thinking about?" Perhaps he had seen something. Stone thought he was on the verge of shouting, and then the head turned and the priest looked at him.

"I've been dreaming," he said.

"Curtain says you must drink this up. It's tea-time. There's a biscuit as well," he picked in the tin.

"You've been sick again I can see," said Stone, staring at the old man's feet. "That's because you won't eat anything, Father Michaels. You must eat something, this biscuit –"

The priest's mouth opened wide, like a fish, he shook his head.

"My teeth," he said.

"Drink this up. Do you good."

A hand reached out for the tin, and Stone held it to his mouth.

"There," he said, listening to the other's heavy breathing, the slobbering sounds, "surely he's much more than seventy, he's very old."

He couldn't hold the tin to his mouth. A feeling of horror seized Stone, he was afraid of the priest being sick on his hands, and then he was hating himself for harbouring the thought, all the seconds that his fingers gripped the tin, whilst he watched the chin bob about, the hooked nose partly disappear down the tin, "How slow he is." He turned his head away, and the horror was gone. He thought of Curtain, watched Curtain tending this old man, feeding him, making him comfortable, stripping him, massaging him, cleaning his face, his dirty, trembling mouth.

"I'm bloody silly," he told himself, and the tin fell to the deck, a thin streak of white splashed. Father Michaels was finished.

"I believe I'm getting better," Father Michaels said. "Have I been very ill?"

"You were, on and off, it's the boat, we've all been sick, except him. But look how beautiful everything is now," he said, enthusiasm behind his utterance, a hand waving past his head. "Curtain was quite right, yet at first I didn't believe him. Now he says the weather will get warmer. He's been in these situations before. He knows."

"I'm not really ill, you know. Just tired. When I look at the sea for a long time it makes me drowsy, then I fall asleep. I see the great ordering of waters, and if I listen intently I can hear the sea breathing, it is so quiet, so quiet. Can you hear it?"

"Yes," Stone said, watching impatient fingers rubbing at the mouth, as though the old man were endeavouring to rub it away, something he was tired of, hating it. His trembling mouth.

"Where's Gaunt and that other man? I can't remember his name," he paused, then added, "Fix this."

Stone took Curtain's vest from behind the old man's head, shook it out and refolded it, made the pillow more comfortable.

"Lie down flat, you'll be all right."

"I can't. It makes me dizzy. It's the sky. Sometimes I look along the boat and it doesn't appear to be moving. Where is Gaunt? What is that young man's name. I can't remember, something wrong with his foot."

"Benton. Both feet are swelled now, he can't walk."

"Oh dear! I wish I could stand up. I've been sitting here all the time, lying here. I wish I were well, I keep falling asleep always."

"Curtain says you're going to Ireland when we're picked up."

"Oh yes, yes, I'm going home to Ireland, that's right. Will Curtain come along and sit with me?"

"Yes. He's rowing there. Look! He's the only one who can do it properly."

"I wonder how far we've travelled. Miles and miles and miles perhaps."

"I don't know. He knows. He knows everything."

"He doesn't like Gaunt. He told me. But that's wrong. Gaunt's a poor, weak creature. No more than that. You know about his wife. I've been thinking a lot about that lately. Something wrong with his head. I can't recall seeing her on the *Aurora*. Probably drowned. Poor woman. How selfish people can be. What a small world contented him. He told me a lot about himself. Now she's gone and his money's gone, home and business. Everything. A son in Canada. Sad, sad."

Hearing a noise Stone looked round. Curtain had drawn in his oars. He sat quite still, listening. The eternal see-sawing sound had ceased. He could not remember a silence so sudden, so deep as this. Even the sea seemed soundless, the boat gliding smoothly through water, helped by a stern breeze. Standing up, he looked down on the priest's bald head, the grey hairs blowing in the wind. He was going home to Ireland.

"And me for the Midlands," he said, getting up and walking slowly away. He saw Curtain standing with the tin in his hand, looking down at the two men. He heard his name mentioned, cried, "Wait a minute, wait a minute."

"What's up with you?" asked Curtain.

"He can't row. He can't even stand up," Stone said, pointing to Benton.

"He can sit on a seat. I see nothing the matter with him. He's had a good rest. Two men can't do all the rowing. Gaunt here, too. Nothing wrong with him. They have to take their turn like the rest of us. No turn, no ration. I've just told them that."

"Give me mine," Stone said, hand stretched out. "God! I'm so thirsty –"

"Drink it slowly," Curtain said, "you two men better cut along there," nudging Gaunt with his foot. "Come on."

"I tell you he can't row," shouted Stone, "he can't, I tell you."

"He will row," Curtain said, "it's my bloody life as well as theirs."

Bending down he lifted Benton up, carried him along and sat him down, called to Stone, "stand by this man here. Make him row."

He went back to Gaunt.

"Come on," he shouted, "I've had enough bloody nonsense here."

VII

"YOU'RE FRIGHTENED," CURTAIN SAID.

"I'm not."

"You're frightened," Curtain said. "You're a rat."

"I'm not frightened," shouted Benton. "I'm not," the blood rushing to his face, his whole being throbbed with protest.

"Shut your mouth. I told you to keep away from that man," Curtain said. "You're frightened, and the old man isn't. That's the difference between you. Stone was frightened, too. Once."

They were seated opposite each other, Benton's swollen feet dangling, ugly under him. He was hot and tired, sweating, his arms ached, his hands were blistered. Curtain's eyes never left him.

"I told you you could row," he said. "You can row. Better than any of us. That's better than lying around like a mongrel dog, isn't it? Only trying to do the best for you. Your girl in Somerset won't be any more excited than my missus when she hears I'm safe. And don't go imagining things that aren't there. Upsetting people. Yesterday I was looking at you lying there and I said to myself, 'Lumme, nobody'd miss you if you went over the side.' I like that priest better than you. And listen," pressing down on the other's shoulders, "when I first

88

dragged you fellers off that rope you were no more than dead herrings to me. I couldn't even see who the hell you were, it was that dark, then my mate got killed, and then in the morning I saw you all and you didn't look tuppence to me, and that's telling you straight."

Benton studied the black bearded face, the heavy chin, the open shirt collar, the red, scarred neck.

"You didn't believe I was right, did you? You told the others a lot of damned lies, didn't you?"

"I didn't. I was scared," Benton said.

Benton remembered things very clearly, even coming down the rope in the darkness, falling in a heap, being sick, waking when the light came, seeing the sailor standing there looking at them all. Remembered his name being taken. He had been a little afraid then. It had made him think of being drowned, his name in a book. He couldn't swim, he'd be drowned. His name would be in a newspaper. Dead. He remembered rowing with Gaunt after the sickness had passed, his feet in water for a long time, heavier than lead, trying to pull him down, down. Sitting with the priest, seeing nothing but water, even clouds appeared to him as though they'd fall into the boat and turn them over. How they would all be in the sea, swimming, trying to swim, seeing in the midst of all this a house in Somerset, his girl crying. He remembered Gaunt talking to himself as he rowed, shouting out in his sleep. His head was badly cut, the sailor had bandaged it up. He didn't remember hearing Gaunt say, "If we drown, he'll drown, too," meaning Curtain.

He looked down at his feet now and laughed. "I'm not afraid, I'm not afraid," he kept repeating in his mind. He wondered why his feet had swelled, he thought of the gargoyles he had once seen outside a church in Somerset. Quite suddenly the oars slipped from his hands. He was in Somerset.

He was lying in a blue bed, in a small low-ceilinged room. It was cool. The curtains stirred as the wind passed the trees. It was quite bare, and its whiteness was like the walls. He stared up at the ceiling. Everything was still, he heard nothing save the voice of his mother talking below stairs, talking about him being afraid of cockroaches. He heard his father laughing then.

"It's so silly to be afraid of a cockroach," his father said, laughing again. He stared up at the ceiling. He would close his eyes, open them quickly, as though to take the ceiling by surprise. But it was still there, it hadn't moved, it was still white. He would watch this whiteness fade as the evening grew, watch it grow grey, then black. He would stir uneasily in the bed, hear them still laughing at him because of his fear of cockroaches. He stared now but he could not hear anybody laughing. They had gone out. He wondered where, and looked round just to see if they were in the room all the time, unknown to him, spying, watching, ready to pounce and laugh in his face, telling him not to be silly. Cockroaches could not harm anybody. They would not nibble at the ceiling, it would not fall down on top of him and kill him. Once or twice he turned his head, just to make sure they were not there. Quickly he would look up at the ceiling, suddenly afraid it might move. He did not want it to do anything but remain quite still, cool and white, so that when he had looked at it for a long time the whiteness would press down upon him and he would fall asleep. He liked to fall asleep that way, pressed into it by the whiteness above his head. Once he thought it did move, float about, something big and white and flat. He watched.

Something might crawl along the whiteness, a beetle, a cock-roach. It was a battlefield bare of soldiers, clean and white, like a field before the guns went off and the soldiers charged each other, and the air was quiet, there were no cries of wounded. He kept opening and shutting his eyes. He was certain his mother and father had gone out. If they had, it would be strange that they didn't say anything to him about it, and his mind cried, "Are you out?"

The curtain moved again and he turned quickly, looking at it. Suppose the cockroaches started to come down the curtain, and along the walls, and so to the ceiling. He would lie there hot and frightened, one might fall off, slither down inside his shirt. He began to shout, his voice made circles round the room, breaking down quietness there, came back at him, saying, "Ssh! Ssh!"

He listened. He thought they were already moving down the curtain.

"What makes you so afraid of them?" his father said. "It's only an insect."

"I can feel them on my face," he said, "as soon as I see one I can feel it on my face I tell you," his mind racing, "on my face, on my face."

"You're a silly little boy," his father said. "A cockroach is only a thing," his father said, drawing the sheets over his shoulders, pressing them in round his neck. "You'll get cold."

He thought of those things looking up at the ceiling, which was cool, beautifully white. A beetle there would be a mark, like a boot covered with mud, smearing it. He had to watch that, if he saw a beetle on it he would shout down to his mother.

He watched, tense in the bed, thinking something moved

across it, then the curtains blew in again, making a swift, soft shuffling sound, and the sound crossed the ceiling, he heard it cross, he thought a shadow passed over it, too.

He shut his eyes, saying his prayers, after which he would say ten times slowly, ten times quickly, "Nothing on the ceiling, nothing on the ceiling."

He closed his eyes, he opened them. Something moved. His mind raced, words tumbled over one another, scattered, got lost, he dived after them, caught them. His lips moved fast, "Nothing on the ceiling, nothing there."

It moved. Small, black, it moved, swelled in the middle, stretched, legs spread-eagled, it crawled. "Mother," he shouted, "a cockroach – quick!"

Slowly he drew his feet up in the bed, knees pressed against belly, feeling his belly's warmth against them, his hands cold. He hated them, they made him sick, he could not look at them. It crawled, a smear spreading, swelling, still swelling, it might burst. He shut his eyes, drew the sheets over his head, cried in his mind, "Go away! Nothing on the ceiling, nothing on the ceiling, mother! Mother!"

Words tumbled, rolled about, rushed this way, rushed that, he couldn't grip them, his lips moved quickly saying nothing. His face was hot, his hair was moving on his head, it might be wind. He sat up, scratched his head. It had dropped on to his head. He wanted to scream – his mouth would not open. He wanted to look up; he flung the sheets over his head. The room was hot, growing smaller, the ceiling trembled. "Nothing on the ceiling, silly," he said, "a cockroach is only an insect, God made them – but it's silly."

The cockroach spread, grew, he could see its head, and eyes green, many legs hanging from its body. It was climbing. It thought it was on a wall, climbing. The bed creaked – he was shivering. "Mother! Mother!"

"At seven you oughtn't to be such a silly boy. Suppose an owl came in and sat on your pillow you'd be frightened then. Go to sleep."

She kissed him, her mouth was like ice. The door banged. He hid under the clothes: he could hear the cockroach moving. "Count ten slowly, ten quickly, go to sleep. The cockroach isn't there, isn't there! There! THERE!" eyes staring up at it. It had covered half the ceiling. Its body rose up and down, and he could see the breath coming from its mouth, like a mouth in wintertime when the snow hushed things and the ceiling glowed with its own whiteness. The cockroach talked. It had a tongue. It talked, "Bigger, bigger," it said.

He lay quite still; he could feel the blood racing through his veins. The room was getting dark with the black thing on the ceiling. It breathed darkness against the white walls. It looked at these. It said, "I am coming down, down."

"DOWN! DOWN! Mother! Dad, there's a cockroach on the ceiling. I'm frightened, frightened."

The door banged below, snapped to: he thought of teeth snapping on the ceiling. The cockroach had turned, its head hanging. It looked at him. It looked through the white sheets. It saw him. "Coming down, down."

He sweated into the sheets, he gripped the collar of his pyjamas, twisted it tight about his neck, he would keep it out. "It's coming down."

The cockroach ran. Its hundred legs stretched out, pawed, clung. Its blackness spread. He could not see the ceiling, it was gone. "Count ten slowly, count ten quickly, shut your eyes, open them, it is gone."

He opened his eyes slowly, the hands clutching the sheet shook, his hair came over the top of the sheet, his forehead, slowly his eyes, fear full, bright like one in fever, face pale. "Mother! Mother!"

Wanting to jump, not jumping, wanting to scream, throat closed, wanted to dance on the bed and was still, cowering, frightened – the cockroach was looking at him, eyes half-closed, sleepy looking, tired after crossing the ceiling.

"There's no ceiling, Dad – Dad!"

"That child is really naughty," his father said, "he wants a dose of liquorice."

"Count ten slowly, count ten quickly, nothing on the ceiling, nothing on the ceiling." The tired words fell down, heaped in his mind. The cockroach fell, the sound was like a great rush of air. He did not look at the ceiling, he listened, it was crawling, hundred legs crawling. It would climb up the bed-post, fall on the sheets, crawl to his face, smother him. Terror laid him still, held taut the sheets, made his heart thump. He was afraid of cockroaches. They made him sick. In school he left the room, he had to go to the lavatory five times in one morning.

The cockroach sat up, crossed its hundred legs, watched him. "Coming!" the cockroach said, "Coming."

He heard it talk. Things didn't talk. His father told him that. The cockroach talked. And then it fell. The bed shook, the noise was like thunder in his ears. His eyes were open, he couldn't shut them now.

The cockroach was as big as the bed. It moved like a snake, wave-like, like a worm, twisting and turning, its flesh was blue and grey, like a fish he once saw his father catch in the river. Its back rose high, touched the ceiling, two columns of air came from its nostrils, he could see them clean against the ceiling

94

which was still white. The blackness was gone. The curtains were still – it was getting darker now. It was on one foot – it was on the other. It was heavy, like lead, it was growing all the time. It would fill the room.

The cockroach smelt like shrimps he once picked on the shore; it had a sea smell. "Ten quickly, ten slowly, go – go."

He was sat up in the bed: the cockroach was under him, he could feel it. It rose up, he was on its back, it moved across the bed, it soared up to the ceiling, it clung there, he was being crushed, the strong smell of its blue skin came to him, his hands pressed the ceiling, his mind raced again. "Count ten quickly, it will go. Count ten slowly, it will fall." His bed was not there, he couldn't see it. The cockroach moved towards the window – he was on its back, clinging, shouting,"Dad, Dad, Mother!"

The cockroach fell, and water sprouted up. The oar struck Benton clean in the mouth. The cockroach was moving in the sea. He screamed out, "A submarine, a submarine." The water had drenched him. "Submarine, submarine," he screamed, wiping his face. "Quick, quick, Curtain! Curtain! Submarine," and he flung himself out of the seat, staggered on swollen feet towards hands that were already reaching out for him.

"Easy there, son! Easy there! You have been dreaming. That's no submarine, it's a whale, I've just caught sight of it myself."

He threw an arm round Benton's neck and held him to him. Benton was shaking against him now. "Got a shock I'll bet. They do have that look. "But just look," he said, "just look," his finger pointing abeam. "Lovely," he said. "Whales are lovely to look at – like children. It's playing, see! Look how that water spouts up from his snout, high into the air. You never saw a whale below – then sit down here with me and just watch. That's no submarine. A submarine wouldn't know how to play.

Not like that. Gaunt, Stone, wake up there. Come and see the whale – come and see the whale. Tell the priest there, it's a whale, a whale," his voice full of an almost childish enthusiasm.

Gaunt and Stone brushed past him, they stood together, hands on each other's shoulders.

"Good God!" Stone said, "just look at that, Gaunt."

"A whale," Gaunt said, "a whale; I heard somebody shout submarine. I got really scared."

He sank down, dragging Stone with him.

"Father Michaels!" shouted Curtain, "Father Michaels!"

The old head turned.

"Whale, whale!" shouted Curtain, making fantastic gestures with his arms, unexplainable to the priest, staring at him, wondering. "Whale," his mind said, slow, uncertain, "Whale, whale." "Over there! Look!" and Curtain jumped up leaving Benton there and went for'ard and sat by the priest.

"A good sign," Curtain said, "a good sign. Never seen a whale before, Father Michaels. Look at it. Can you see?" his hand behind the priest's back, raising him, the old eyes searching, searching for the whale.

"That thing moving," Father Michaels said, suddenly short of breath, "that . . . "

"That's it," Curtain said. "My little daughter is always asking me if I have seen a whale and I tell her plenty. See how it plays in the sea, Father," Curtain said, his voice loud, as though afraid the priest would not hear him. "Just like happy children. And that fellow Benton gave me quite a shock at first shouting submarine, submarine. Guess he'd been dreaming or something."

They watched, so friction melted. They forgot, care went, water smiled at them – they were quiet, watching. The whale plunged, rose, danced on smiling water.

VIII

THE SHAPE GREW UNDER their eyes, rose higher in water; so this wilderness was broken by a whale, the silence struck out, the whale tossed water high in air, it drew nearer to them.

"Beautiful!" the old man said, "beautiful!" – fascination changing to fear, "Will it sink our boat?"

"No! Don't worry." Curtain's words like ropes safe round Father Michaels. "It might if it got a chance, but they do no harm to anybody, and I don't think it will do harm to us. It doesn't like boats no more than it likes men. The sea belongs to the whale, belonged to it first and will in the end," Curtain said, unaware of shapes moving in Father Michaels' mind – Jonah stirring in the depths there, under dust from pages of books, under piles of words.

"A sailor always likes to meet a whale. Some say they're unlucky, but I wouldn't. You wait – to-morrow we'll see something else," and he began to laugh as though the others in the boat had never been with him, only this old priest staring like a child at the enormous whale.

It was like a light come into a dark room, a house risen in the great desert, a world looming up, peopling the sea, sending out warmth to them in their little boat. It was like the sun after a year of darkness, grass and flowers after acres of black mud. Thirst was gone – hunger gone – bad blood gone – while the whale plunged and rose, tossed and turned, and water churned, danced higher, higher, the noise like voices speaking to them.

The whale was not in Curtain's mind. There was a single bird there, wings fluttering, waiting to be free. A bird winging over great stretches of water, high up, hovering over their little boat. It made the smell of earth come into his nostrils, touch of known things already in his hands. It made him hope, forget all that had happened, suspicion and stubbornness, disgust and impatience sank out of sight. Only the single bird was in his mind: he could vision it setting off from a high cliff, moving far out to sea, wheeling and turning, sweeping and gliding – one single bird – the thought of which made fierce for a moment the clutch on Father Michaels' arm.

They sat there, but did not speak – just watched – their eyes could not tire from watching, that, through hours, stretching to days had seen nothing but the emptiness, the indifferent sky, the monotony of slow, of swift moving waters.

"By God! It's coming our way," Stone said, "it might swamp us," turning to look at Curtain who did not move, but watched with the priest.

"It's all right, it won't harm us. Have a good look at him before he goes," shouted Curtain, and Father Michaels was saying in his ear how wonderful it was for him who had only read of these things in tomes and sermons.

"Jonah and the whale," the priest said, "I think of that. But what an enormous creature."

"Yes, a kind of sea elephant." Shouting behind him, "What d'you think of the whale, Gaunt?"

"It's amazing," Gaunt said, "so near to us."

Back on his seat Benton thought, "Was I dreaming, or what?" Looking about him, as though he had just wakened from a long sleep. "I saw it first, too. Funny – I must have been dreaming – I thought it was a cockroach," laughing to himself, "Mother and Dad looked up life-size: how they used to chaff and torment me about cockroaches when I was a kid. I suppose I was scared. I was dreaming," patting his knee, hardly noticing that the oar had gone, vanished for good in swift running water. "I was dreaming I was at home in my little room at the top of the house." He thought of his girl, too.

Curtain came back and sat by him. At once he saw what had happened. "Christ! Benton," he said, "What have you done with the oar?"

"Oar? Oar!" Benton said, his girl dancing about in his mind. "Oar!"

"It's gone," Curtain said, and Benton looked up – his girl gone, flashed out of his mind as though this man's words had thrust her out. "It's gone. Oh hell, gone, gone," and Benton looked about, a little frantic, a little afraid of the tone of Curtain's voice, the whale forgotten.

"The oar! Were you asleep or what? How the hell did you lose it? It's like losing a man losing an oar. I wouldn't mind if there'd been plenty, but trust a boat to have everything in it when you come into a bloody fix like this."

"I'm awfully sorry, I'm really sorry, Curtain," Benton said. His face burned with shame – he could hardly glance in the man's direction. "It must have slipped; I can't remember anything. I don't remember losing it. I was rowing, and then I saw that whale – I mean I thought it was a submarine. I saw it before anybody."

What were they going to do now? Curtain did not speak, but Benton read it in his face.

"I jumped out. I got excited, goddam it. I am sorry," he said, his hands clasped together on his knees, like somebody on the point of kneeling down in prayer, a foolish look on his face.

"It can't be helped," Curtain said, "it can't be helped. But it means we've only three oars instead of four. Ah well!"

"I say there!" It was Gaunt shouting. "The whale, this damned whale!"

"It won't do any harm," shouted Curtain, "I've already told you that. Don't worry about it. Just sit there and watch it playing – you won't see another whale like that for years if you ever see one at all. Stone, come here."

"Anything wrong?"

"Yes, lots – almost as bad as if the whale had rammed us. Benton here, he's lost the oar. We've only three. Now what?"

Stone looked from one to the other. "Hell!" he said. "Hell!"

"It's a bull," Curtain said; "yes, I'm sure it's a bull."

"How far off is it, about how far?" Stone said.

"A mile – little more," Curtain said.

It rose slowly in the sun, shining, sank into abysses, and water boiled. It turned, its bulk lessening, it blew. The fountains of water caught the light, descended like fire, and the whale was gone. They could not see it. Eyes searched the water.

"He's gone."

"No he hasn't, there he is – look!"

Hands pointing, "Just there."

But they could see nothing, except a patch of disturbed water, and then his tail moved, ponderous. He rose again, carrying ocean on his back. Flooding him. It poured away, it vanished once again.

"They always play like that," Curtain said. "You watch; soon he'll come up behind us."

They waited. The boat rocked. No-one rowed – no-one cared – there was a whale to watch, its size staggering all but Curtain who said quietly. "But we can't stand here like this," and he went and picked up the oars.

"He'll be behind us in a minute," he said, seeing the look of concern on Benton's face, who thought he might row the boat slap in the whale's direction. "Don't worry about him, just watch him play. It takes their minds off things," he reflected, "that's everything, taking their minds off things."

He rowed strongly now, like a man who was rested well after good food, his mind clear. Their backs were to him, they stood or sat, Stone and Gaunt whispering to each other.

"If it had been a ship, hell . . . " he heard Gaunt say.

The whale had come up astern now; to the watching men it appeared to have grown twice its size. It was mountainous. It dived, it swam, it rolled, it turned, its tail cleared water, caught the sun, an enormous propeller. Sometimes it blazed as though it were carrying the sun on its back.

"Will it roar?" Gaunt said.

"I don't know, I wish it would," Stone said.

And Curtain rowed away from the whale, not thinking of this now but of the lost oar, "Bad luck," he said, "damn bad luck."

Father Michaels watched, hand to his eyes, watched the whale, but Jonah was sunk into the depths of his mind again, covered with dust of sermons, many thousand words. He watched a mountain that had been washed into the sea, lost, rolling about in the depths, coming up to surface again, heaving and tossing, and these as spreading far, far, and he thought of loneliness, of the great heights, great depths, and once he wondered what his eyes would see if once these waters should part. He put the other hand to his eyes, the strong sun beat down on them, he followed every movement of the strange animal in the sea. He thought of it as a life, lost, wandering, always alone. He wondered what its eyes saw beneath the surface. The spouts of water fascinated him; he watched the whale with half-open mouth. Sometimes it seemed to him to race forward at great speed as though bound for some particular destination, and then he knew there was no destination in the ocean – the ocean was but a vast circle of waters, the great order of waters never changing – never tiring, never still. The whale lived in these, surrounded by wall upon wall of silence.

Benton, Gaunt and Stone had gone aft to watch. It still played about within sight, and they sat down together, not looking at each other, not speaking, simply letting their eyes follow each movement of the grey and then fish-blue convulsion in the water. The sun flashed on its back, water poured over it, streamed off like a waterfall, its great tail appeared to spin in the air. Its bulk slowly turned, the big head came up. Fascinated they sought for its mouth, and saw gusts of foam, water shooting up, waves rise and curl, fall flat, waters part, the whale sink into the trough created by the wave. They forgot they were in the boat, forgot Curtain rowing, forgot yesterday and the day before, as though doors in their minds had suddenly shut down.

The whale was further away now, its back looking like a thin line of light, and then it was gone. They watched on, but nothing moved. Disturbed waters fell back into order again; the surface shimmered under the light of the sun, but the waters were not disturbed again, all was as silent as before. But their eyes did not tire, but looked on, searching this stretch of water, now that, unavailing, and then slowly there came to their ears not the sound of down-pouring fountains, but the slow monotonous sound made by Curtain's oars. And as one man they turned their heads and looked his way, seeing his broad back, upright, his arms wide-spreading, his hands hidden.

"He's rowing," Gaunt said.

"Yes," Benton said. "We're moving along," as though the sight of one man rowing towards a skyline that danced with light were a miracle to see.

They sat there looking at him for a long time, as though this were surprising. Curtain, a stranger, suddenly come into their boat.

It was the noise of the oars in the rowlocks that broke through the world of the whale. And it seemed to Gaunt as he watched that Curtain had been sat like that since ever he could remember, rowing, rowing, an everlasting man rowing over sea that had no end and no beginning.

"He's been rowing all the time," Gaunt said.

"Course he has; Christ, we have to move, haven't we?" cried Benton.

"That's it, we have to move. I forgot. I was thinking of that whale. Just imagine it swimming, swimming all the time, never stopping, in the daylight, in the darkness . . . "

"Stone!" Curtain called, "Stone!"

It turned the key upon an hour that had been full of light.

"Stone! Come down here. Can't you hear me calling you?" Curtain shouted.

When he left them, Benton said, "I lost the oar," looking up at Gaunt.

"The oar?"

"Yes. Curtain cursed me to the devil, but it wasn't my fault. I saw that whale before anybody," pride in his voice, "and I got a hell of a fright. I saw it a long way off and I thought it was a submarine."

"A submarine," Gaunt said, "what a mind you have, Benton."

"But it wasn't, after all, only a bloody whale," Benton said, laughing. "But he's mad with me. He said he'd rather a man was lost than an oar."

"He said that?" Gaunt gripping the sleeve of Benton's coat.

"Not exactly that, I mean, well he said it was just as bad as losing a man," Benton wound up, and slowly went away, leaving Gaunt standing there with these words spinning in his head. They were like ladders upon which he could climb, look down into Curtain's mind.

"What a funny thing to say, rather lose a man than an oar."

He went slowly up the boat, past Curtain rowing, past Benton and Stone, and sat down by the priest. Curtain hardly noticed him; he was talking to Stone. Behind them sat Benton, thinking of but one thing – the lost oar.

"Were you scared when Benton shouted that time?" Curtain said, low in Stone's ear.

"Yes, I'll admit I was. I thought it was a submarine."

"And it was just a harmless, playful whale," Curtain said, still speaking in whispers, knowing Benton was behind him. "I'll tell you something, Stone. I'll tell it just to you, because you're sensible, and I can rely on you. When I saw that whale my hopes rose. I said to myself, 'A whale, what does that make me think of?' It made me think of a bird. I said to myself, 'I'm sure that we'll see a bird soon – doesn't matter what kind of bird it is – it'll be a bird, and it will come suddenly out of the sky, hovering over this boat,' and that means land, Stone, land. See."

Stone gripped Curtain's sleeve. "Land," he said. "Land," quickly, and the word was beginning to swell up inside his brain. "Land!" he said. "Land."

"Yes, but for God's sake don't shout, will you?" Curtain said.

"You really mean land," Stone said, excited now. One foot made a sudden rattat on the boat bottom – his mind crying, "Land, land."

"When you see the first bird you know everything is beginning to look all right. Look at this bloody ocean, just water, rolling along, humming along, going anywhere, going nowhere. Think of a bird, and then everything's different. Things have shape, meaning. Understand? You're moving towards land."

"Oh God!" Stone said under his breath, staring at Curtain whose face was in profile, watching his eyes and wondering if the sailor was not now, this very moment, searching the sky for the bird. "Bird, bird," he said quickly in his mind, "Bird – land." He leaned on Curtain, words came in a burst, "We might see a ship then?"

Curtain nodded, was silent for a moment. "Might see anything," he said, and he pressed his foot on Stone's toe as though he were steadying something in Stone, excitement growing in Stone – it must not burst out. He had to think of the others. He spoke again. "This is only what I think," he said, "I wouldn't say a word to the others, because it would go to their heads. I daren't excite them any more. I have to think of to-morrow.

"To-morrow?" Stone said, "to-morrow?"

"Yes. Water will be less to-morrow, biscuits just as hard,

two each if anybody wants them. Say nothing to the others about what we've been talking on. The least thing will upset them now," and then so softly that Stone had almost to lie on him, "this fellow behind is ready to go off at a touch. He's all worked up about the oar. I was mad, goddam the position is bad enough."

At that moment Benton got up, looked at Curtain, then went for'ard to sit with Gaunt and the priest.

"You see," Curtain said, raising his voice a little, "I had to tell him off. It was so bloody silly getting excited like that. An oar's everything to us. Your water may go, but you have an oar and can use it while you breathe, and I told him off. Thought he saw a submarine. I really believe he thought he saw a bloody submarine."

"I was talking to Father Michaels just now, and he's changing, too. He never mentions ships, never seems to care, as though this was something quite permanent now."

"You lose count of time."

Stone was feeling Curtain's back. "You never dried your clothes."

"They are dry – dried on me. Never noticed they were wet. Never noticed they were dry. Just look at Gaunt there holding the stage again. I suppose he's pouring out his miserable tale to them. Benton is a curious chap. So easily influenced by Gaunt. They've been talking about me. They think I don't hear them, but I do. You hear everything in a little boat. Funny, talking about boats. Always I used to say to myself, I wonder what it'll really be like having thirty-two human beings in a boat, and you've never set eyes on them before, and only one other sailor with you, perhaps two. I've been in this situation five times now, and I never yet had a full complement."

"You talk as though you were disappointed," Stone said.

"Am I hell!" Curtain replied, laughing. "Show me your hands, Stone."

Palms upwards, he showed his hands to Curtain.

"Um!" he said, "Um! Blisters. Sore?"

"Not now," Stone said, his voice a little weary as though he were tired of the talking.

"Sure you feel all right, Stone? The same thing happens tomorrow, don't forget that. Don't count on anything I say. One talks a lot of nonsense in a boat, especially after two or three days."

Stone was swimming in doubt, and clutched Curtain's arm. "Blast you," he said, "you were talking about a bird. You must be crazy." He went on shaking the man's arm. Finally Curtain shook it off and said, "Don't be a bloody fool – you take chances, goddam, it's all chances now. You have to talk about something, even a little bird. It passes the time away. And who are you to say there mightn't be a whole cloud of them. You saw a whale to-day: why the hell shouldn't we see a bird to-morrow?"

"You said we *would* see a bird. You said it to me. That kid was listening."

"I said nothing of the bloody sort. What I said was this," letting oars drag, facing Stone, placing two large hands on his knees and pressing there as if he were expecting the man to jump into the air. "I said it raised my hopes, nothing more than that. Now let's not talk any more. Know what the priest says, don't you? 'Time to talk, time to be silent.' He's wise, Father Michaels is." His mind said, "Switch off, quick, switch off."

"I thought we'd lose him all right," Curtain said, "I really did," eyes on Stone's eyes, holding him, "I thought he'd die."

"Thought who'd die?"

"Why, the priest of course. Now it's somebody's turn," he said – shouted, "Hey there, Benton! Hey there, Gaunt! What about a bit of a push on the way home?"

"And for Christ's sake don't see another submarine," Curtain said, as Benton sat down, "what were you talking about up there?"

"Duck eggs," Benton said, eyes roving over the boat.

"Makes me feel hungry, doesn't it you, Stone?"

"I don't feel hungry," Stone said, "only my eyes ache looking at the damned sea."

"You're not tired enough. When you get really beat your eyes won't ache, Stone, your bones will. Come and stick your hands in the sea. Nothing like it for blisters. You got any blisters, Benton?"

"No!"

"Course not. Look at that, Stone," he said, "there's muscles for you. He'll be a man when he steps ashore out of this boat," and he dragged Stone after him.

"You don't take notice of anything I say, surely. After all, lumme, I have as much right to talk rot as you have, now haven't I?"

Stone sat on a seat aft, leaned over and put his hands into the sea. He let them hang heavy, watched them drag through the water, as Benton rowed.

"After all," Curtain said, "we just can't sit looking at each other like a lot of stuffed dummies, can we? If we didn't talk then we might all go barmy. I don't take any notice of the gabbling of that fellow, Gaunt, even that wife of his may be an invention. You have to talk about something. Father Michaels has been talking about duck eggs. That makes you feel hungry, and you talk about big dinners you'll have when you get out of this. Come on, Stone, you kept up your spirit fine all along, don't get shaky now. Things are beginning to settle down to normal again. The priest is a little better. Gaunt's even lost his sulk, Benton's forgotten his feet. Cheer up, hell we're not dead yet," and he began slapping him on the back.

"I was only thinking of the bird," Stone said turning, but not looking at the other, only seeing Gaunt there, talking. The priest sitting motionless, a carved figure silhouetted against the skyline. You looked this way and one was looking at you; you coughed and an eye was on you; you lifted this hand and then that, one was watching you. You spoke, all were listening; you breathed, they heard it. The boat was full of eyes, waiting, watching. Stone felt them on him now.

"They know we've been talking about ships again, being found, picked up."

"Don't be a fool. They can't hear you. What makes you think they know I was talking about a bird? Nonsense. It's so easy to get yourself worked up. It only makes it bad for yourself in the end. You lie down but you don't go to sleep. Your brain gets full of ideas, you get hold of something quite dotty and hang on like it was a matter of life and death, and you don't sleep. Hanged if you do. Be like me, Stone."

"Like you?"

"Why not. Think of a bird you might see, and go to sleep on it, but don't let one bird become thousands, so that you toss about and can't settle down at all. Take it easy. I'm bloody sorry I mentioned the damned bird now."

For what seemed an age they were silent and finally Curtain left him standing there, carrying with him the same uncertainty

in his mind. He cursed himself for talking about a bird. To hell
with the bird. "Christ, you must talk about something, something."

He came up to Gaunt and the priest. For all three the whale
rose in the ocean again. It was gone, but only temporarily.
Father Michaels spoke, and there it was on the surface again.

"That whale was enormous, Mr. Curtain," he said, the "Mr."
forgotten, came back to full stature again. "Mr. Curtain, I've
never seen a whale in my life, and I was so glad to see it
that I told myself it was worth being in the boat just for that."

"They're quite harmless," smiling, "so long as you keep out
of their way."

"Makes you think a man could be swallowed quite easily
by one of them," Gaunt said. "Quite easily. I've read about
them, I never thought I'd see them," his face so calm, his
voice so quiet that Curtain told himself that Kay was worlds
away, forgotten. Gaunt was coming back to normal; Gaunt
was becoming himself, something he must have been long
ago. Gaunt was really better now. So they talked of the whale,
shape and length, colour, its weight and habits, all three talked
of this quietly, coolly, like three professors in a laboratory.
"Now the age of this whale, I should say it was about . . . "
talking like this as though nothing had ever happened in
their lifetime but catching sight of one lone, playful whale.

You had to keep cool. This was being cool. Curtain was
certain now, more certain of things coming right for them
than ever before, not worried with to-morrow, nor water, nor
people being sick; thoughts were cooled in the mind, the
signal was up, there was no danger. Like a river quietly
flowing, straight on, no creeks, no reedy swamps, smooth
flowing. Their lives were like that at this moment. Only a

bird flew about restlessly in Stone's mind, one oar hung in air for Benton, one cockroach became a submarine, and then a whale. He thought of Father Michaels breaking biscuits on old, green teeth, Gaunt singing as he rowed, Benton with his boots on again, sitting quiet as a mouse, Stone behind him, cool, certain like himself.

The day was long, air quivering with heat, the light hard, sky brazen. He never thought of darkness, when always this had lain in his mind, and thoughts circling it like warning signals of danger. A man over the side, the boat flooded and upturned, Father Michaels crying in his sleep, Gaunt sneaking to the water, head jerking, watching, hands on the keg. He did not think of these now. To-morrow was like a clear day. Somewhere the bird flew, somewhere it sat on a high cliff, wings fluttering, waiting to take off, wind whistling up the face of the cliff, and then it flew out with a quick crying sound high into the air, making for the ocean, as though it knew the boat was there, and one man rowing, rowing towards the land. The bird carried him away – he did not hear the priest asking him a question which Gaunt answered.

"Yes, that's right, there is not much water left," he said.

A gong struck in Curtain's mind. "Relieve that kid, relieve him. He can't do it. Go ahead. I've been rowing most of the time. Go ahead."

Gaunt went. Curtain looked at the priest. The bird was gone, winging downwards to the sea.

"I don't think there's any need to worry, Father," he said. "We've enough for you."

"I only asked; it didn't mean anything, really," seeing the curious expression on the sailor's face. "I just wondered."

"There's enough for everybody," Curtain said, "enough for

three whole days. Don't worry. Everything will be all right. I promise you that," patting the old man's hands.

"Three days," he said. "Three days. Lots can happen in three days. Just think, you might be safe and sound then, lying in a nice cool bed, and lots of . . . Three days?" he said again.

"Yes, three days," Curtain said.

You could not keep silent. You had to talk. Even about water. You had to talk.

"Has Gaunt been talking about this to you, Father Michaels?"

"No, no! He didn't talk about anything except the whale. He used to talk to me about his wife, but he doesn't now, and I'm glad. It was tiring, and it was all so trivial, I thought, so trivial."

"Was he talking about the water, that's what I want to know?"

"No!"

"All right, I'm satisfied. You see everything is fine now. No nerves in the boat, nobody thinking the worst has yet to come, nobody wondering, just talking nonsense about whales. It makes it easy. You aren't worried. Now I'll bring you a drink," he said.

"Going down, down," he muttered as he looked into the keg. "About two days at the most. There's milk. They'll have to have some of that."

"Only one danger now," he said, "drinking the bloody ocean."

He went back and gave the priest milk and water mixed. "Drink this, it'll make you feel fine. Then sit quiet. Soon you'll fall asleep. Try not to think of things, forget everything. I'll come and make you comfortable before it gets dark."

"Where are you going, Mr. Curtain?"

"Along there," pointing aft, "there, where the shelter is."

"What are you going to do?" asked Father Michaels, spilling the milk on his coat and making a long white line there.

"*Sleep*!" Curtain said. "Go fast asleep, I don't know how long it is since I was asleep."

"Can't you sleep?" clutching Curtain by the coat, "You're worried about something, Mr. Curtain."

"About nothing," he said, "I was thinking of that whale. It was funny to me, the way it danced about in the sea. They play like that."

"You're worried," he said, trying to stand up, falling down again. "Worried."

"Not me," Curtain said, and went away.

IX

A DAY PASSED, NIGHT came, this passed: so the boat crawled, an insect in this ocean, flat, soundless. Silence was great arches under which it passed, and high above a sky, watery blue, pencil-lined by light flecks of cloud. The eye travelled and stopped at a line where sky and water met, where one patch of water danced, one line of light seared the heavy shadow of sea. Zenith of power was reached and the eye withdrew, trembling; it closed as the circle of ocean began to spin, dizzied, it lost its power. One listened, and breathing was thunderous. One sat, one lay, one sprawled, one's mind was water-washed. One ransacks ocean for a moment, hope spirals upwards, doors close, locks turn, hope spirals down. There is nothing in this ocean but one crawling boat.

Outcircling this ships move, a world of ships, through lanes, round headlands, past points of rock. Ships pass ships, join sea to sea, round capes, sheer off points of rock, lay to, plough or go astern. They speak with each other through air electric, ships speak by eyes, light blinking to light. Wave speaks to wave, this ocean is alive. They hide in bays, move through shifting darkness, restless like clouds. They move above, below, one's wake is calm, one's wake is frenzied, ships attack. Ships pass through light and darkness and hours are struck upon a bell. They search each other out, they watch and wait. Ships move, cunning slow, only alien waves show speed, light mirrors science's wave. They prune all surfaces of sea, ships move below, down reaching, shuddering near to hell. These oceans rock, these oceans never cool. They move in line, purpose to purpose chained, one circles these aware, far-watching, wake threshes wake. Ships plan to-morrow before to-day is old. Light trembles on these shapes, some towering high, some squatting low, these seas alive, but no eye sees one single crawling boat on this dead ocean where hours are laid low, as low as hope, a lurking claw to spring upon one single sight or sound, one crawling boat upon a flattened sea. Ships sing to other ships, too far to hear, ships move towards hours that have a certainty.

Light touched their eyes, soft, like fingers. They stirred together, body close to body, Gaunt and Stone. Slowly waking, half out of dream, weariness, their eyes opened. They looked at each other but did not speak. The sky yawned down at them.

"God!" Gaunt said, "God!"

Words formed in Stone's mind, his mouth opened as though to speak, but the words could not pass over the burning bridge in his throat; his mouth and tongue seemed full of little curling flames. He half sat up, but a wave of inertia passed over him, pressed him down again.

"Hell!" Stone said, "Oh, hell!" And then he sat up. He felt weak, his feet were leaden.

Gaunt sat up, too.

They looked around, and saw Benton lying with one arm thrown over his head, and the priest's body bent into a half circle. They wondered if the two men still slept. They did not notice that the boat was drifting, that Curtain slept amidships, his body slumped like a sack, drenched in sleep.

"My back aches," Gaunt said, " . . . aches."

"I can hardly stand up," Stone said, standing up, pressing on Gaunt's shoulders with his hands. And then he saw Curtain.

"My God!" he said, the words forcing their way through his hot, dry lips. "Something's happened to Curtain," and clumsily, painfully, he made his way towards the sleeping Curtain and began to shake him.

As he shook the heavy body his terror grew. The boat was drifting, but how long, how long?

"Wake up, Curtain! Wake up! Curtain! Curtain!"

The man's body rocked under Stone's shaking hands, to and fro across the seat.

Gaunt was now behind him. "Wake him up!"

Stone looked at Gaunt, said nothing, went on shaking the sleeping sailor, a frenzy in his hands a feeling of utter emptiness within him.

"He's not . . . " Gaunt said.

Stone went on shaking Curtain. "Wake up; Christ, wake up, Curtain," whilst messages telegraphed through his mind. "Only he knows, knows. We can't do anything without him," Stone spat this in Gaunt's face.

"Does he really know?" Gaunt said, fear and caution intertwined, his eyes resting on the face of the deep-sleeping man.

"He knows. We depend on him. He knows . . . " Stone said, furiously, his mind crying, "Knows how far the land is. He knows," Stone said, "he told me. He goes by the stars at night. His watch . . . his . . . wake up, Curtain." He went on shaking the apparently dead sailor.

The ocean expanded in their minds, the ocean was the world, it squeezed them in. Together they slumped down into the seat and stared stupidly at the sleeping Curtain.

"God! will you wake up?" Gaunt shouted in his face.

He rowed when they were sleeping. He talked to them; he helped them; he tended to the priest when he was sick; he massaged Benton's feet; he laughed at a whale. He said, "Keep cool." He said, "Everything will be all right." He talked of a bird, he talked of humpbacked waves, he watched for the land swell. He knew. He was there, always. He gave out water, soaked biscuits, forced them into an old mouth. He said, "So long as you keep cool then everything will turn out all right." And now he slept. They had thought of all these things, certainty in their minds. Curtain was there, always. One shut one's eyes, one opened them, he was there. One was sick, he was there. And now he slept, deeply, and they had not thought of that. Terror linked terror.

"Good God Almighty! What's wrong with him?" Stone swung a hand in air, like a pendulum. "He's worn out, we never thought of that." He leaned forward and began shaking Curtain again.

Gaunt sank back upon the seat, weakness pulled him down, but he tried to stretch out one foot, tried to kick Curtain awake, but the foot would not reach. Suddenly Curtain was not there, he had vanished; there was only a water keg, lying at Stone's feet, and Stone's eyes were upon this. Slowly he turned his head round and looked at Gaunt. Waves of heat circled his half-open mouth.

"Gaunt!" Stone said in a half-frightened whisper, "Gaunt!" Then he looked down at the water keg. "Gaunt," he whispered. "Gaunt!"

The keg was growing bigger under his distracted eyes; it floated about in front of him, and a slow grin passed over his face. The keg was an eye looking up at him, a watchful eye.

The keg was Curtain's eye, staring back at him.

"Gaunt!" Stone said, "Gaunt!" He grabbed his hand and pulled him into a sitting position. He whispered in Gaunt's ear, "A drink?"

"He's asleep," Stone said, "he won't know. One drop each."

"One drop," Gaunt said, the pupils of his eyes dilated. "One."

"Just a drop each," Stone said, his hands trembling downwards towards the keg.

"But quick! He'll wake. Only one drop. It's our ration anyhow."

"The tin," Stone said.

"I don't know – damn!"

"Where is it?"

"Up there!"

"Where?"

"By the priest. I saw it."

"Get it," Stone said.

"No, you! I can't move. Oh hell, my back, my back . . . "

"Get it," Stone said, his eye on Curtain's eye that covered the keg.

"We don't want a tin."

"We do, damn you," Stone said. "I thought of it."

"Ssh!" Gaunt said, and put his hand over Stone's mouth. "Listen!"

They listened. Curtain breathed heavily, his head pressed down on his chest. For'ard a head turned, small blue eyes looked down at three men sitting amidships. Benton turned over on his back and groaned.

"Quick," Stone said, "For hell's sake, Gaunt! The tin! The tin!"

"You get it," Gaunt said.

"Blast you!" Stone got up, and made slowly towards the priest.

Gaunt leaned over, endeavouring to pick up the keg, his hands were over it, then suddenly he drew back, his eyes fixed on the sleeping sailor's face.

"One drop. Just one drop," he cried in his mind. "It's our ration. One drop."

But he did not move. Doubt seized him; he thought he saw Curtain open his eyes and look at him. His mind cried, "Hurry! Hurry!" His tongue was swelling in his mouth, he was choking, flights of coloured balls danced before his eyes. Curtain was suddenly still. Gaunt's hands were on the keg. He watched Curtain's face. Gaunt fortified himself.

"One drop! Just one drop! It's nothing . . . my bloody throat."

These words were girders holding up resolution that had begun to waver. Curtain fell on his back, arms stretching wide; he snored. Gaunt almost cried out in fright when Curtain tumbled backwards; he made hoarse noises in his throat. He looked for'ard. Stone was standing with his back to him. He saw him bend down, one hand thrust out, his head was a little to one side. The hand remained in air. Stone was hesitant. He seemed to be watching Father Michaels whose head was almost touching his knees. Whilst Gaunt stared, Stone moved. He was looking back at Gaunt. Eye met eye, that spoke to each other by silence. Gaunt made frantic gestures with his arms – Stone signalled back to him. Noiseless Gaunt gripped the keg, lifted it up, pressed it to his breast for fear it might fall, watched Curtain, flashed looks at Stone.

Erect now, clasping the keg to him, he could not move. He wanted to go forward with the water, his mouth moved as though he were going to speak, but only the top of his tongue touched parched lips. Something held his feet; iron clamps. He made a desperate lurch, he was free. He did not know what held him; he knew he was free, and slowly he staggered for'ard with the water.

"That's what he meant," he muttered. "That's what he meant. Bring it up . . . there."

He saw Stone bend down to pick up the tin; the water was already in his mouth, ice cool, he could feel it washing round his tongue; he scrambled over a seat, nearer to Stone, nearer to the tin.

"One drop," he told himself, "just one single drop. I've got it," he said, "got . . . it," stumbling forward.

He would have dropped the keg but that Stone reached out and grabbed it. "Ssh!" he said, "Ssh!"

"The tin," Gaunt said, and sat down, short of breath, hands gripping the seat.

They did not think of Curtain sleeping, no drifting boat was present in their minds.

"The tin," Gaunt said, "blast it, the tin. Only one drop each, Stone, one drop. No more."

"Ssh!" Stone said in a furious whisper, for the third time bent down to pick up the tin that was lying in the bottom of the boat at Father Michaels' feet. How it came to be there he did not know; for one brief moment he imagined that in the night the old priest had had some water to drink. The tin lay by his left foot. Suddenly he drew back as though he had been struck, stared vacantly at Gaunt.

"My God!" Gaunt said, "can't you get it, are you afraid?" Reached down for the tin, went sprawling, but he grabbed the tin.

"Ssh!" Stone said, "Ssh!" Pinched Gaunt's arm, his eye on

Benton turning over on his back. "We don't want him here, too," low in his throat.

Gaunt did not know how long he lay there, sprawled, tin in his hand, his mouth moving, grotesque, comical. Stone wanted to laugh. Gaunt righted himself. Father Michaels was looking straight at him, piercingly with his quiet eyes. He did not speak. He simply looked at Gaunt who lowered his head. The priest looked at Stone, and Stone turned his head away.

"What's the matter with him?" Father Michaels said quietly, eyes watching Benton coming forward on all fours. Stone saw. Gaunt saw.

Stone spoke, spat in Gaunt's ear, "Damn you, you woke him, too."

"Who?"

"Him!"

Gaunt looked, gave a little laugh. "I once had a spaniel named Peter."

He put down the tin, picked up the keg.

"No," the priest's eyes said, "No!"

"Gimme a drink," Benton said, "drinking it all yourselves. Bastards."

"One drop," Gaunt said, "only a drop, it's our rations."

"No," the priest's eyes said, "No." He leaned over, pressed his hands on Gaunt's knees.

"My throat's on fire," Gaunt said. "You have a drop."

The priest waved his hand. "I'll wake Curtain," he said. Benton was on his knees. Stone rocked on his seat; Gaunt held the keg. He held them there; they could not move. They were like a sculptured group. Slowly he shook his head, his eyes said "No." Surprising them, he stood up, he felt his body as light as air.

"I'll wake Curtain," he said slowly, looking from one to the other of them.

"We're lost."

"He doesn't give a damn."

"No," Stone said, "No, he's dead beat."

"Don't touch that water," Father Michaels said. "I ask you, please not to touch that water." He spoke to Gaunt, and Gaunt shouted loud.

"Damn! I can't stand it," lifted the keg up, held it there, watching them all.

"I'll wake Curtain," Stone said, looking at the priest.

"Yes, wake Curtain," Father Michaels said.

"You won't," Benton said standing, arms out, gripping Stone. "He wants a drink, so do I. Nobody gives a damn, I've been lying there . . . "

They struggled together, their bodies hid Gaunt from view. He started to pour water into the tin. Benton fell against him; the water spilt.

"Gaunt!" Father Michaels said, "Gaunt!" and was knocked down as Stone and Benton struggled in the bow of the boat. He could not speak, the wind was out of him.

Amidships, Curtain slept, deep exhausted sleep, his body like a log, his trusting mind slept too.

"I'll kill somebody," Benton shouted, "Gimme that water, Gaunt."

Two became three struggling bodies. Father Michaels could not move. The boat rocked in the quiet waters.

"Please!" the priest said, words coming slow, "you'll drown us all. Please! In God's name, Gaunt."

Stone fell, Benton fell, struggling at his feet. Gaunt drank from the tin.

The boat rocked, nosedipped, water came in, she heeled over.

"Gaunt!" Father Michaels said, trying to reach for the tin. "Don't be worthless, Gaunt," saying this was sick, turned his head from them, leaned on the gunwale of the rocking boat.

Gaunt drank, and then the tin was knocked from his hand. He cursed and looked at Benton, his tongue out, eyes lolling, he looked like a dog. Gaunt laughed. His shaking hand endeavoured to bung up the keg again; instead it beat a tattoo all over the wood; finally reached the hole, he pressed on it, then his body took the weight of the two struggling men.

Father Michaels vomited over the rocking boat. Stone stood on the tin, squashed it flat under his boot. Benton tried to reach the water keg. Gaunt tried to stand up, fell down again.

"No!" the priest said, between groans, "No!"

"Look out, my God you'll have it over," Stone shouted, hitting out at Gaunt, knocking the keg to the bottom of the boat. "You'll have it . . . "

Curtain slept on. In dream he drank for a wager, glass after glass, seated at a table, ringed by men, all laughing, shouting, taunting. Glass after glass went down; he burst out laughing. "You can't do that." He climbed a tram with Mum, Nell's hand in his, she followed.

"Come on, old girl," asthmatic puffs in front of him. They sat. They climbed the tower, watched Mum blow, waving down to her. Nell laughed. "The shute!" she said, "The shute!"

"The shute!" he said, still holding hands. They sat down, and she between his knees; they whizzed through air. His body rocked from side to side; laughing in Nell's ear he said, "Makes you dizzy, kid."

And then he woke. The boat rocked, the shute was gone. Nell gone. Mum gone.

"Hey!" he shouted. "Hey!"

He sat up and then he saw them struggling.

"My Christ," he said, and went hurrying towards them. "My God," he said, "all three."

They heard him come, stopped dead, turning round. They watched his face.

"Blast you, you lousy bastards, what's all this?" Hands on his hips, he looked at them, they quieted down, they gasped like fish. "You thought you'd have some when I fell asleep," he said.

They did not answer him; they lay there very still; he heard Father Michaels being sick.

"You lousy lot of swine," he said, as if talking to the priest.

He sat and looked at them. You fell asleep, they pinched the water. You couldn't trust them, any one, you trusted your own brain and nothing more.

He kicked at Benton, "Get out of here," he said.

"And you get out, too," he said to Stone, "I trusted you."

"What's the matter here," he said, surprised by the quietness of his own voice. Trust had you guessing all the time. "What's the matter here?" Pushing by Gaunt, not caring where he went, into the damned sea. He saw Father Michaels sick.

"Sick again?" he said, laughing without humour. You couldn't trust anything but your brain.

"It was the boat tossing, it started me sick again," old mouth, mouthing air, "I thought it would go."

"What?" Curtain said, it was like an ultimatum.

"The keg; I told them not to touch it. I tried to shout. You were asleep."

"A few minutes," he said, "one has to sleep."

He picked up the keg, saw the tin smashed flat under Stone's feet.

"What the hell's the matter with everybody?"

Benton's face stuck out at him, his mind saying, "What the hell is this?"

Then when he looked round, Gaunt and Stone were gone. He felt deserted. He was in a street, knocking at every door. "Is this the place?" No, not this, higher up. From door to door, so one went on, unsure, lost. "Try this door." "Not here, try lower down." He was like that, lost; he couldn't trust them any more.

"How long was I asleep?" he said.

"A long time. I didn't know till now. They woke me up, arguing among themselves. I thought Benton was quite mad. I was afraid, but I knew they wouldn't touch the water."

"I'll get the baler," Curtain said, and turned away down the boat, passing by Gaunt and Stone. He came back, emptied some water in from the keg. "Here!" he said, "You drink this."

He was curt; this priest was no priest now, only a man, old, but still a man. You trusted your own self, nothing more. "Drink this up," he said.

Like a child, the priest raised his mouth and drank. Curtain went away. He put the keg back where he had last left it, then sat down. He took no notice of the other three. He picked up the oars and began to row. He would not wait long; they would come to him. He knew; was certain.

The boat glided through silvery sea, the boat was full of the deep, strange smell of the sea.

"I wonder how long I was asleep, I wonder," the phrase jumped up and down inside his mind. "How long was I asleep?"

"It wasn't me!" He looked up; Benton was standing by him. "Sit down," he said.

"It was Gaunt," Benton said. "It woke me up. Christ, give me a drink."

"All right. Sit tight. No shouting out of you." He gave a drop of water to Benton and said, "That's got to last a long time. Who woke you up?"

"They were fighting down there. I was asleep."

"Drink this. Shut up. Then go and lie down again. There's nothing else to do."

He took the baler from his hand. "Now be quiet."

He knew they were watching him; he knew they would come up, one after the other, looking for their ration. He saw Stone coming first.

Stone sat down, but did not look at him. Curtain went on rowing, rowed as though Stone were not there, had not existed. You had to trust yourself. He was talking to Stone before he quite realized it.

"It happened once before, and it was Gaunt. Who was it this time? I don't care two hangs, it's your life, not mine," his dead, heavy eyes on Stone.

"It was me," Stone said, "I took water from the keg."

"You did?"

"It was me," Gaunt said, struggling up. "It was me."

A torrent of words blew up at Curtain; he could not understand. He thought of three Chinamen talking, a troop of monkeys chattering.

"What?"

"It was me. My God! How long is this . . . "

"That's it of course," Curtain said, "you don't trust me – none of you. Even he is doubting now," pointing to the priest.

"No, no I took the water, Curtain, my mouth was burning, I couldn't . . . "

"My mouth is burning, too. And now there is no water," Curtain said.

"No water?"

"No! There was before I fell asleep. There is enough for the priest in the morning," Curtain said. "You see what happens when you don't keep cool. Well, there it is."

They looked at him, stupid; he thought of faces under pipes, grinning in a stall, a box of coconuts standing in a ring, he taking aim at these faces in a row, smashing them to pulp. Five hits and a miss.

"Christ! Don't stare at me. I'm not the prophet," he said angrily. "You brought it on yourselves. You let me sleep. You didn't care a hang. I could kill you for taking that water – Stone, go away," he said.

They mouthed at him, eyes in hollow faces under matted hair. An incredible rage seized Curtain, filled him with sudden strength, like an unsought revelation, and he shipped his oars. Listing one high above his head he brandished it as though to strike them down. Salt water drops fell down the blade, splashing their faces. Great veins stood out on the sailor's forehead; he glared like an animal from eyes half-hidden under bushy brows.

"Go away, you sods," he shouted in their faces. "You bloody crawling lot of swine. Get into the stern there and bloody well stop there." He swung half round to the priest. "That goes for you, slobbering old fool. Sit down, the lot of you, and stay where you're damned well told."

His voice cracked like a spark out of his swollen throat; he retched violently as it seemed to close his gullet altogether.

He slumped in his seat, the brandished oar trailed now in the glassy water beside the boat.

Gaunt, Benton and Stone sat down; they sprawled, lolled. Stone's feet stuck out in front of him, swung about slackly to the movements of the boat. They did not look at Curtain. They did not look at each other – they looked at nothing, feeling nothing.

The shock of Curtain's shout in the sea silence numbed them as men are numbed by the cataclysmic event.

Hours seemed to pass, until at last Curtain appeared to rouse himself once more. He sat up freed from the torpor, said so quietly that he hardly heard his own voice speaking.

"Benton, take an oar."

Benton made his way to the seat in front of Curtain, with a grotesque stiff movement, and took up the oar. They rowed. They rowed erratically, without rhythm, aimless, purposeless. Then down the boat floated a bubble of sound, and Curtain looked. Father Michaels was on his knees.

"Praying," he said, "praying."

He felt a pressure upon his eyes, his mouth opened wide, like a dog who waits for the bone that will be dropped into it; it looked like a grin, frozen, the bared teeth shone white against the black of beard. He breathed heavily. Still the bubble of sound floated down to him; he remembered a pilgrim ship, voices coming across a bay, hidden choirs in holds of ships, hot air, sweltering. His foot started to itch, he rubbed one boot against the other. He remembered a dark grey quay and pouring rain, grey hides rising in wet clouds from hazy holds. A word in his mind – anthrax. The bubble of sound floated past him. He did not move.

Sometimes Benton's oar would be pointed upwards, and the

water ran down the blade on to the leathern grip, making it slippery so that he found it difficult to hold, and it turned in his hands. Sometimes his blade would skim the top of the water, dashing bright showers of spray towards the two in the stern. The rowlocks creaked, oil-less.

Curtain grunted a little as he rowed, and this was the only sound other than the faint chuckling of the wake under the stern of the boat. Curtain watched Benton's back. The back of his neck was young still, thin like a boy's neck. Seeing this, dullness in Curtain's mind thawed a little, the rage that rose from looking at Benton's back cooled. This was only a lad. A kind of fierce pity held him for a moment. There was exhaustion in this neck, in the long, lank hair that hung tousled over Benton's forehead, in the weak hands that had once sculled a little boat along the Thames.

Time passed like the slow waves and slower clouds.

"Get off now, Benton," Curtain said. "Gaunt, take Benton's place."

Benton fell forward and pulled himself along the sun-dried flood boards.

"I can't, I can't," a strangled whisper in the throat of Gaunt.

"Take Benton's oar," Curtain said.

You had to trust your own brain, no world existed outside of this. It was your life.

They rowed. The sun sank lower and lower towards the horizon. A faint, slightly chilly wind ruffed the water, and the light faded slowly to a leaden grey. Twilight was like sadness coming down over the sea. A nullity between light and darkness. In the bows Father Michaels snored. Time passed.

"Stone!" said Curtain.

The name was like a thing in itself, a stone dropped into the stillness of a great pool. Stone and Gaunt changed places without a word.

They rowed. Slowly the night lifted itself skywards, the light in the west thinned to a line, and then faded out altogether.

Curtain, of instinct, through the fog of his weariness, watched for the stars. They came inevitably. One here, one there, familiar as faces, welcome as friends, cold and cool to the eye. He knew them all. He knew their names, the bright parts of the machinery of his life. They pointed the way.

"All right," he said to Gaunt, and shipped his oar.

Gaunt went on rowing. He had heard nothing, was beyond hearing, seeing.

"All right," said Curtain again, "d'you want to row in circles?"

He pushed Gaunt sharply in the back. He fell forward on his face, and lay in the bottom of the boat without moving. Curtain shipped the oars and got out the sea anchor. Very slowly he let it down into the water. It seemed of extraordinary weight. He could barely lift it. The rope slipped warmly through his hands as he paid it out. Quietly the boat swung round, sideways to the slight swell. The inert bodies rocked in the bottom like corpses.

At last she hung stern on, the rope grinding a little where it was made fast. The day was over, the darkness was complete.

X

"GOD!" CURTAIN SAID, "GOD!" He pulled on the rope. "Christ, I'm getting weak."

He pulled again, his hands weakened, he sat down. He stared stupidly at the infernal rope. It held the weight of the ocean, of the world. Again he pulled, it moved, he held on, not seeing, not thinking, only feeling the rough rope against blistered hands. He leaned over, dipped one hand in the water, moistened his face, he kept his mouth tight closed. "God!" he said, "God!" and then it came.

The weight sundered, scattered, he pulled, pulled, and so went staggering back and fell, the rope tight in his hands. He lay there, stretching one foot, stretching the other, his bones cracked, the first shivers of early morning passed through his body. He did not look up, he looked at the rope resting on his breast, he looked at his hands. He had slept, woke, slept, woke, in fitful starts, in shivering bouts. He could not see the sky, the sea, he could not see the other men. He only saw the rope upon his breast. Slowly he sat up and looked about. He looked at them. Quite still, things. Like oars, like ropes, like framework of this boat. Things. He pulled on the rope, he stumbled towards it as it came. It was done, it was in. The boat was like a fish, caught, held in the hand, a throb electric shot through it from stem to stern. He turned and looked at them again. He looked at the priest, whose arms were folded and his head pressed on them, his bald head like an egg, white shining against the drab of clothes.

Curtain dragged himself along the boat and picked up the baler. He leaned over the side, one hand holding on to the seat. He filled it. "I'm weak," he said, lifting it into the boat. He grabbed it with two hands, went and stood by them, the things. He half turned the baler to pour water over their heads, he spilled it down his clothes. The baler fell to the deck with a clattering sound. He bent down to pick it up, knelt, pressed his hands on the seat, rested there. His head was heavy; he wanted to let it lie on the seat. He knelt in the water he had spilled, he felt a murderous burning in his mouth. Very slowly he reached down one hand and picked up the baler. With great effort he leaned over the side of the boat again, half filled the baler, raised it clumsily, tilting it, large drops splashed, he lowered it down, poured the water over Benton's head. The thing did not move. Curtain rested. Laboriously he leaned over again and filled the baler, his hand weakened; hand and baler struck the side of the boat, water splashed on Gaunt's face. He did not stir.

"I'm weak," Curtain said, "I'm not weak." Again he dipped the baler, he christened Stone, watched water run from his hair, between his eyes, hold in its flow in lines run deep each side of Stone's nose. He let the baler fall.

"I'm not weak," he said, "not . . . " He crouched a moment, humped like a cat, looking at their faces. He was resting again. "I'm not weak, not . . . "

He went forward slowly, moving like a crab, the baler dragging in one hand. He dragged over a seat and clung there, baler dangling. He fell forward on the priest who did not move.

The baler fell from his hand; his mouth pressed against a button on the old man's coat. He rested there, not seeing, not hearing, not feeling anything but rest. He raised himself up, eyes on the priest.

"Dead!" he said, "dead!"

The word was as deep as the ocean, weight of ocean.

"He's dead," hands moving up the coat, towards scraggy neck, colour of old parchment, fingers moving up, touching his filthy collar, moving up. Touching his childish face, feeling flesh, not white, not red, not carrying blood, an old face, dead.

"He's dead!" he gulped, "dead."

He ran his fingers round the mouth, shut tight like a purse, up both cheeks towards eyes, black ringed, tender veined, he touched his nose, "dead." He lay on the priest and forgot. He lay on the priest, saying, "Dead, dead."

You rose trusting, you went down trusting; you believed in a bird. Trusting, that was your life, outside that nothing, a void. You trusted your own life and nothing else. You could not trust a man, a stormy sea.

Warmth was on his face like breath, and slowly, like weights, his heavy lids rose, and his eyes saw trembling on that face, mouth opened like a fish, and air come out, the nostrils quivered, and Curtain stroked the open mouth, he stroked the forehead, ran fingers down the cheeks, mouth to priest's mouth, eyes to trembling eyes, he saw life quiver under transparent lids. He saw a tongue gone yellow lie on old teeth.

"I . . . "

"Oh, Christ! Good Christ!" Curtain said, his fingers moving over the priest's bald head.

"Am still . . . " tongue moving, chin moving, lids fluttering, veins dancing over them. "I'm still alive," strength spent in words, breath creeping out, breath warming Curtain's fingers.

"Alive," he said, "alive."

He stroked his face, his mind cried out, "Alive."

He touched the eyes, lids fluttered up, he saw the priest alive.

"Ssh!" he said, "Ssh!"

"I'm still alive . . . all right," the trembling ceased.

"Don't move," he said, "I'll bring you something now."

Curtain's body sagged, like a sack he slithered down at Father Michaels' feet. Then he raised himself up and made his way towards where he knew the water keg was lying. He went dizzily, his mind was swimming towards the keg. He sat down, suddenly, like one who has travelled far, and now forgotten the purpose of his journey. It was his head, his feet, pulling like lead. He did not know how far he had travelled, whether it were mountains to be climbed or spiral staircase winding into dark, he did not know he was looking at the keg. He did not know how long he was sitting there. He had come far, far from a dead priest, alive. And then his fuddled mind took wind, was slowly cleared by this. He saw the keg. He looked at it for some time without moving. Then he put his hand down and touched it with the tip of his finger, he pushed it this way and that, tried to press his finger on the water hole. He bent over and lifted it, it hung in air, he dropped it with a crash. It had an effect in his mind, an enormous wheel, fast revolving, whirling sounds, and then it suddenly stopped. He could feel the stillness after the crash.

"Hell," he said, "hell." He didn't remember the priest, only the crash in the bottom of the boat. Movement pained him, movement was an effort, climbing a mountain, hoisting the ocean on a rope. He gripped the keg again and held it, slowly lifted it up. It dropped on his knee, he clutched it to him. Its weight had a steadying effect upon him, like iron bands circling his body. He fiddled with the bung, and finally with clumsy fingers, broken nails, he got it out. He bent over and with one eye, he looked into the hole. Darkness. He peered into it for a long time, he lifted it up, shook it, something rattled at the bottom. "Some in it," he said. He forgot the tin squashed flat; he remembered the baler. It lay by Gaunt, by Stone. He put down the keg and got up again, staring round, trying to remember. Then he knew. The baler by Gaunt and Stone. He journeyed off again, stopped suddenly dead – "I'll carry the keg," decision broke, like wave on rock, he dragged himself along, he found the baler and picked it up. Then slower than before he journeyed back again. He sat down heavily, wiped clean the baler with the sleeve of his shirt. He stood the baler on the seat, it balanced precariously, he lifted up the keg. He looked round as though eyes were watching him, eyes he could not see, he listened for a sound. He turned over the keg and water trickled out. He watched it spill in drops into the baler, the baler seemed huge to him, a gigantic bath.

"That's it!" he said. He thought he heard his own tongue cracking inside his mouth like a whip.

He fiddled with the bung, like Gaunt; the hole was lost, he banged it on the keg, he couldn't find the hole.

"Hell! There!"

It was done. Gently, as though it were a child, he put the keg down on the boards. Then he picked up the baler and slowly made his way for'ard to the priest.

Half-way he stopped; the baler held out in front of him, suppliant, like a beggar with a tin. Had he bunged the keg?

He wasn't sure. He hesitated, round his mind a signal flashed, "Have you bunged the keg?" a question he did not answer, feet moving blindly forward like a diver's under sea. He remembered the priest, stumbled on, careful of the water in the baler.

"The others," Father Michaels said.

"Drink this," he said, his arm around the priest, his arm holding one man of God.

"The others," the old man said, "the . . . oth . . . ers."

"What others?" his mind said, "what others?" eyes wide upon the baler. "Please drink this, shut up, will you, shut up, drink this," holding the baler to the old man's mouth. "Put your tongue in it then," Curtain said. "Here! Hold up," and then he forced him back, secure in the crook of his arm, put the baler to the old man's lips, felt pain in his shoulder holding up the priest. "Come on, Father Michaels, drink this up."

He watched him drink. It sounded like a horse's muzzle in a trough; a grunting pig, fly-covered cow mouthing in a pool, green slime, on summer's day. He watched him drink.

"All up," he said, "all up."

Hands pushed against the baler, pushed it away, "Enough . . . the others." The mouth shut.

"I said all up," Curtain said, hoarseness in his throat. "Enough for one more in the keg," he said, dipping his tongue in the baler, licked glistening drops, inviting there. "You'll live, you're all right, you'll live."

"Thank you," the old man said, lay back, shut eyes, joined hands, mind wandered off.

"I'll make you comfortable," Curtain said, lifted him up, straining.

Eyes opened wide again, he saw a longish boat, some seats, an oar, three stretched-out men.

"A battlefield," Father Michaels said, closed eyes again.

So Curtain's arm was free and he got up, went slowly back with the baler in his hand. He stopped again to lick the baler dry with his hot tongue. His lips said, "Ah . . . "

He sat rubbing the shipped oars, one hand on each, like these were bodies, flushing them to life, by pressure of his hands, fingers against wood, he went on rubbing them up and down, feeling stout leather there, his body see-sawed thus. Water was like oil, thick sluggish water, gobbling at this boat, a furry mouth. His hands were still, his face upon an oar, delicious, cool. He dipped his hand in water, moistened his dark face. He leaned hard over, cupped water in a hand, baptized himself, feeling water cool upon his burning head, something sang within, a tagged tune, a tune he did not know. He looked at his smashed watch, its crazy face showed twenty minutes and two after twelve o'clock. He put it in his pocket, and picked up the oars; his arms began to move, the ragged tune was gone. His mind expanded then, dark corners lighted up, he watched a patch of cloud move slow and curl, melt as he looked, he watched an empty sky.

"Not dead," he said, "I thought he was. But them . . . " and turning looked at three, head touching head, one foot stuck out grotesque, jutting from the boat.

"All this on top of him," he said, eye sweeping sea, and Crilley on his mind, risen up from dust, as quick as light, as large as life, "all this on top of him."

Far below and cool, he would remember him, flat out upon a keg, a body bullet filled. He trusted and went down, a trusting man.

"In the name of Jesus Christ."

137

These words he heard, a murmur in this boat, he raised his head, and then he saw the priest upon his knees, and watched him there.

"I thought he was a goner and he's not."

He rowed, the oars flashed, great waves of heat struck down. He half-closed his eyes, and faced the sun, saw travelling beams of fire ride down; he bowed his head. At last he shipped the oars and sat quite still. He watched the sky meet sea, half-circles, emptiness, he watched the nose of the boat bob up and down; he watched a kneeling man, he thought of Nell, of Mum.

He was in fo'c'sles breathing fetid air, he was in dock counting minutes on a clock, he was with others pulling on a rope.

"I wonder if he'll die, if he will . . ." and slowly he was slipping down, down, so crumpled up, straddling dry boards.

"Jesus!" he said, "my mouth."

He did not remember slipping down, nor how long he had been there. Somewhere, far off he thought he heard the tinkle of a bell; it struck in his mind, went on ringing there. He dragged himself back into a sitting position. A slight mist lay over the water. He put out the oars again and rowed; each pull was long, tortuous, each pull was like a day in his mind, long dragging, grinding. He watched the water, watched the sun. He wondered how far they had rowed, he thought of miles, a hundred, the figures danced about, made him feel dizzy again. And then he saw far out to port an object move. A point or two on the bow. He did not know, he was not sure. He was not sure of this, he sat quite still, increased his grip on the oars, sat forward, tensed. His lips moved, tremulous. He could feel something stirring in him, something deep down, the shout that was to come, the cry to pass through his burning mouth. He watched, he dizzied watching, a patch of water, a circle of light, a patch of mist. He saw the object move. Hardly aware of it the oars had slipped from his hands, his hands were joined together, he kneaded air with them, bones cracked, and then he rose. He put his hands to his eyes, shielded them from the sun. Suddenly he pressed them flat over his face, he did not believe. He believed in a bird, high cliff, these anchored in his brain. Dead ahead the object moved. His whole body trembled, he opened his mouth to shout, a whistle of air came out. He looked again, he saw the object move. A fan waved in his mind, his dry throat was filled with a word. He croaked, "A ship, a ship." They did not move. He clapped his hands, he cried, "Ship! Ship!" He stumbled over the seat, he made his way to them. Kneeling in front of them he shouted, "Ship! Ship!" He slapped them in the face. Gaunt opened his eyes, looked wearily up, shut them again, he heard no shout of "Ship". He pulled Benton by the hair, struck Stone in the face with his fist, cried "Ship" at them. Gaunt turned over on his face.

"A ship! Wake up, a ship!" and then he turned and watched. The object danced in the sun, the object moved down on them. He gripped the gunwale, stared crazily at it. "A ship!" he cried, dragging himself along. He pulled the priest by the coat, "A ship!"

Old eyes looked up at him, old eyes drowned in thoughts. The priest turned over on his side, one eye looked out upon a mist.

"A ship, wake up, a ship!" Curtain went on pulling at his coat, the cloth began to tear, he went stumbling back, "A bloody ship."

The words moved slow in air, floated down to them, but only Gaunt had moved. Raising himself up, one hand gripping the seat. Drunkenly he lay there, staring out. He saw a figure move, grow large by him, larger to his eye, go past. He heard an oak creak.

"A ship! My God! A ship."

No need to wave a hand, no need to fly a shirt, the ship was moving down on them. No need to row its way, it meant to come on them.

"Ship!" Curtain cried, and his mind cried, "Ship, ship, ship, ship, ship."

Stone rolled where Gaunt had been. Benton did not move. Gaunt lifted heavy head, eyes watching nothing, mind still immersed in dream. Curtain sat transfixed, oars in his hands that no longer moved. The object dead ahead, bobbing in the mist. Gaunt pawed the seat, he fell on Benton, slobbered in his ear. The boat went drifting on. The object was abeam.

"Christ!" Curtain said. He rowed. He heard one crawling past, and it was Gaunt. He shouted, "Stop! A ship!"

Gaunt leaned over and now he saw the object move, "A ship, my God! A ship!" He watched the thing approach, his mind returned to him from wanderings over hell.

A tower in the ocean round and grey, flag flying in the mist, a bloated whale, its belly up, shining in the sun. A rounded ship, a great dead fish. They watched. It swelled as it approached, a monstrous fish, a head, a bugaboo. It floated slowly towards them. And then he saw a rubber boat and in it was a man. Gaunt's hand gripped his. The object bumped the boat, and Curtain saw the man. "A man," he said, and stared at it, then shipped his oar, the other one was jammed. He turned to Gaunt.

"You see. A man! Help me, Gaunt."

"A fish."

"A man, and I think he's alive. Help me, Gaunt."

Some strength came back to them; they rose together, hand gripping hand.

"We can pull it in," Curtain said, "pull it . . . in. Grab." he said, leaning over, cried furiously, "not the boat, the man."

They grabbed, they pulled.

"I can't hold . . . "

"Try!" Curtain breathing in his ear. "Try, don't let go."

They pulled again, the figure moved two inches.

"Pull! Pull!"

"Dead."

"Yes."

"No, alive."

"God, will you pull," Curtain said. "Oh, Gaunt, pull . . . "

They held on. Gaunt felt his knees giving way, he lay on Curtain. The head of the man was in their hands. They pulled again.

"Hell, look out, you'll have us over," Curtain shouted, steadiness coming back to him, something calm and reassuring, steadiness that seemed to flow from this dead figure to his hands, so up his arms, steadying him and Gaunt.

"Oh God!" Gaunt said, "it's going, going . . . " knees weakening again, "I can't . . . "

They both went down, kneeling, the figure half in, half out, boat drifting, rubber boat tossing like a cork.

Curtain thought of drowning, he held on. The head was heavy in his arms. He thought of Crilley dead upon a keg. He knew this one, by look and touch of him, he felt revulsion. His mind cried, "Again, again, again."

"Pull, Gaunt, pull, man," warmth going out to Gaunt, not knowing why, feelings going out to Gaunt who had stolen water. "Pull for Christ's sake, will you?"

"My arm."

"Damn your arm, pull."

So his head was cleared of mist, dull dragging thoughts, by sight of one dead man.

"God, I'm pulling," Gaunt said, minded to let go, a thing of death, what good was it, why pull; his mind cried, "Where is the bloody land, where's the bloody land, never mind the man."

"Do NOT let go. You'll go too if he goes. Pull, pull, PULL!"

They pulled together, strength rising up from words, "PULL, PULL!"

The priest sat up, fell back again. Stone rolled about the boat, head struck Benton's head, and he was still again.

"Almost," Curtain said, "almost," pulling the dead weight of the man.

Suddenly they felt a jolt, a fountain of water poured down on them, the rubber boat was free, it bobbed away, the heavy feet sank in the sea. Gaunt let go, Curtain was caught out, the figure slipped, slowly it was sinking.

"Christ, damn you," Curtain said, his arm under the shoulders of the man.

Gaunt spoke, not mad, not wearily, not sulking, not hating Curtain. "Look at him! Look who it is!"

Curtain collapsed under the weight, he went down, sprawling, but he held on to the man. "Quick! Help me – he'll drown."

"Let him drown." He gripped Curtain's legs, began to pull. Curtain did not feel this, weariness was back again, weariness like a cloud, flooding his brain.

"Help me, Gaunt," he said, breathing heavily, holding on. "He'll pull me down."

"Let him go! You see? I see. Let him go."

Curtain felt a sudden pain in his neck. When the world began to swim he shouted, "I'm going, my God! Gaunt! Pull! I won't let go." He twisted his neck and turned, looking up at Gaunt. A frightened man. "For God's sake, I'll drown."

Gaunt did not move. "Let him go."

A figure hopped towards them, rose up and down. It was the priest. He had not walked before, just sat, or lay and stared, dreamed, been sick to death. And now he came towards them, hopping, jerking, like a bird.

"Go back!"

"I'll help," Father Michaels said, put hands on Curtain, pulled, fell dead on him, added weight to weight.

Slowly the figure was sinking in the sea. Slowly Curtain's arms were being pulled from their sockets, and he could feel them tear, sickness, a hollow wind was in his stomach, then slowly his head was pulled, his body started to move again. Far off Gaunt saw a bobbing rubber boat.

"Where is this bloody land, this land," he shouted, and felt a tearing in his throat.

"Gaunt!"

And then Gaunt knelt down, circled arms round Curtain, held, began to pull.

"Leave go of him," he said, quiet, coolness over him.

"I can't, good Christ, I can't."

"He's dead," Gaunt said.

"By Christ I won't!" four words, four gasps from Curtain.

Gaunt gripped the priest, so Curtain slipped again, pushed Father Michaels down.

"You'd drown us all, you fool."

He pulled again – pulled with all his strength as though he pulled a boat towards the land, "the land, where is this bloody land?" as though he pulled at Kay, holding her back, writhing in darkness with a crowd. As though he hauled a tank of water towards him to flood his guts. He pulled, and slowly Curtain came in, pulled and Curtain gathered strength. Father Michaels lolled upon a seat, watching them. He did not speak. The boat tossed, taking water in. He was sick again, sick upon a greenish coat.

"Pull!"

"Goddam, I'm pulling. All this for him."

"Pull."

"A bloody swine like that!"

"Pull!" Curtain said, "Pull!" His mouth was open, tongue hanging out. It caught two drops of sweat.

Curtain staggered back and Gaunt helped him to his feet. He felt his chest must burst.

"Easy!"

"All right, pull!"

Gaunt put his hands on an arm, began to pull. This was the ship, the whale, the bugaboo. This deep sea diver swelling out with air. This balloon-like figure, a pile of rags upon his back, Gaunt thought them rags.

"Again!" Curtain said, one leg pinning Father Michaels to his seat. "Now together," Curtain said. They pulled again, so saw feet rise, stick out like logs of wood, dripping sea back to sea, two legs stuck out like oars, dangling in the air. Slowly they pulled him in.

"Phew! Hell!" Curtain said, failing, carrying the airman with him, an iron cross felt cold against his cheek. Gaunt went down, too. They lay with water from his helmet dripping on their faces.

"Alive," Curtain said.

They eased the weight away; it fell, sank down, flopped over like a fish.

"He's alive," Curtain said, and dragged himself to where the airman lay.

"A German sod," he said, "it's not the first I've seen. Gaunt!" he called, "Gaunt!"

But Gaunt collapsed again and he heard nothing now.

Curtain knelt down and slapped the flabby features of the man from the sea. He put his ear to his mouth. Warmth trickled out; he felt it on his ear. "Alive," he said. He stretched the figure out, unloosened clothes, he dragged off heavy boots, painful to his nails. "A bastard one of those." He slapped his face again, now doubting life, ear to his mouth again. His mind registered a bird, a lone point of rock, the land. Where had he floated from?

"We're near the land, oh Christ! We're near."

He raised his head, he looked out, wondering. "He floated from the land, we're near the land. Wake up!" He slapped his face. "Wake up," his mind cried out, "you sod."

And then he knew what to do. And then he was quite calm, secure again, islanded with hope. "I'll give him a drink, poor bastard."

He left him then, dragged his way past Gaunt, past one old man groaning on a seat. He picked up the baler and stood it by the priest. He picked up the water keg. He took out the bung and poured the water in. He shook the keg, close to his ear. "And that's the bloody lot," wanting to dive in his tongue, wanting to sink his face in it, so near to cool, to fill his drying guts, some drops of water from a rusty baler.

One eye of Father Michaels' opened out on him. But Curtain could see nothing save the baler in his hand. Holding the handle with two hands, slow, cautious, he made his way to the airman in the stern. He trod on the hand of Stone, and felt it soft, plastic to the tread, wondered if he'd died, a curious feeling rose from softness in the hand. He passed by Benton, stopped by Gaunt, afraid. He held the baler still, felt slightly dizzy, made his way, worming round Gaunt.

The baler was the Host and he was carrying it, the priestly eye looked on, then quietly closed. Curtain's coat brushed lightly against the filthy mouth.

"Wake up," he said, "wake up, you bastard."

Breath came from the airman's mouth, and Curtain said, "Alive! He's living."

Slowly he put the baler to the big, fleshy mouth, opening it wide with his thumb and poured the water down, drop by drop, and watched a muscle move upon the whitened throat.

"You'll live, you sod, you'll live."

He raised the empty baler up to his own mouth and laid his tongue in it.

"He'll live."

The baler fell from his hand, slid from the airman's chest. One hand on either side he leaned, then he looked down at the man. He saw Crilley there.

"You may have killed my bloody mate," he said, gave the body a light push, it flopped over, lay still. A dead fish in the boat. Curtain raised himself up, rested a moment, then got to his feet. His heavy eyes looked drunkenly towards the sea. He saw the mist was thickening. He saw Father Michaels roll off his seat like a stone. He made his way along the boat, stepped over Stone and Benton, stepped over Gaunt.

The priest had given a curious tiny cry. Curtain bent down and gripped him by the arms. "Poor old man," he said, half dragging, half carrying him for'ard.

This was where he belonged, a nest beneath the bow, a homing bird. No other part of the boat but this.

"You're all right, all right," he found himself spluttering into the face of the priest, whose eyes opened and closed as imperceptibly as a bird's. He made him comfortable, back against the boat. Then he returned and sat down in his proper place. He picked up the oar, hand groping blindly for the other.

"Good God!" he said. The oar was gone, off with the bobbing rubber boat. He raised the single oar, holding it tight in his hands. His mind was wondering what to do. Something heavy in his hands, an oar. He pointed it, then slowly shipped it, watched the mist rise clear. He sat there, mind drowsed, body like lead, he saw a cloud shut out the sun. He stretched out his arms, leaned back gripping the seat, he saw the sky roll past his eyes. He closed them against the sun.

The day wore on, a slight chill in the air, slight wind behind her stern, the flattened ocean gone, a change of sea, the waters heaved again. He opened his eyes. Blue changed to grey, and a feeling like that of rain in the air. He stared at the water under him. The movements of the boat began to speak to him, language that he knew and then he saw ahead the long grey heaving seas. He fell asleep watching this.

XI

THE PRIEST LAY WITH his head on the boat, joined hands
under him. Lazily he looked at the mist. It was like the fog in
his mind, now slowly clearing. His eyes made a path through
this mist. He saw a rock, and on this rock a man. He knew he
saw this rock, this man. He did not cry out upon the boat, the
object that he saw. He could not cry out, a sound would split
this rock, a sound would rock this man. The mist was slowly
clearing as he watched. An enormous wheel passed, soundless, rolling up the mist. He did not move. He kept his eye on the
rock. He remembered things. He had fallen off a seat and
somebody had carried him here, his own place, where he had
always sat, or lay, been sick, tired to the roots of tiredness.
Sometimes he had gone off alone, on long, quiet excursions,
his mind carrying him over great stretches of sea, and his
body had lain, mindless in this boat. He had reached lochs,
touched quiet rivers, watched reeds everlasting tremble, stood
on altar steps, blessed heads, and once, face downwards, he
floated on a lake. He could slowly turn, look down the boat,
see men lying there, but eyes had ransacked this; he watched
the point of rock, and watching it he saw great rollers moving
up, converging on this rock. The rock was washed by sounds.

He heard these sounds, he even saw them rise as waters rose, surfacing it, like many million mouths, murmuring at its base. The figure did not move, and could not move, he held it with his eye. A point of rock jutting up from sea, a great needle shining through the mist, a finger holding up the sky. The wheel went rolling on, rolled up the mist, he saw it move, move nearer to this rock. He remembered Curtain. He remembered Gaunt. Remembered stolen water. His lips opened and closed, he felt coldness in the air. The boat drifted on, answered to the swell, his body answered this, and still he watched the rock. He thought he saw the figure move, the man upon the rock, then shut his eyes. Shutting them he saw not man, not rock, but Curtain in a rage, Gaunt flat upon his back.

"Too much belief, too much belief in others," his mind said.

He opened his eyes again, he saw the rock. A rock against the ocean. Behind this rock one hid, holding a little grief, against the greater one that flooded a whole world. He remembered a sailor dead, flat in a wooden boat, saw him behind this rock, sheltered from this flood. He heard the sounds again, wash up against the rock, he thought he saw the figure move, he thought it spoke. "One humble grief is hid."

"How pathetically inadequate we are," his mind said; saw rock and figure go, down in a flood. A sea of clamour washed out a world, waves shaped like mouths rushed on. The world he saw was riddled with belief, belief in other mouths, belief in other cries. He saw the rock again, rise from a sea of mouths, a man upon this rock hold still. The music that he heard was clamorous, cries surging on this rock.

"Too much," his mind said, "too much," and then he thought the figure spoke to him, he even seemed to see one finger rise and point at the flood of waters crying round the rock. "These mouths, these mouths."

And if he turned his head he would see an open boat, and figures lying there whose composure was like eyes, blind with trust.

The priest was mumbling to himself, mouth touching wood of the boat, mouth wetting this. But always he kept his eye upon the rock that his eye still saw, far off, vague, still, shapeless in mist. He thought it moved, patches of light and darkness circling it. He shut his eyes a moment, then it was still. He raised his head a little and freed his hands, he tried to sit up, but this brought lightness to his head, and he lay down again. He raised his hands in the air and looked at them. He saw them grey against a light that faded slow like fog in his own mind. He saw long fingers move. He covered his face. He looked through fingers spread, he made the sky a gate. He murmured, "God." He thought his body moved as though by hands beneath, he thought he was falling from the boat, and he flung out his hands and gripped the seat. He felt the warmth of wood, the framework of this boat that carried them through days, through hours he could not count. He lay quite still, he watched the rock draw near, he watched the figure move, upon this rock. The boat drifted on.

Suddenly he turned his head and looked down the boat. He saw Curtain lolling in his seat, shipped oar at his side, one hand on it. But he could not see the others whose names came to his mind, like signposts to an hour he had forgotten. He muttered these names slowly on his tongue as though he prayed. "Stone, Gaunt and Benton – Stone, Gaunt and Benton." Quietly he dozed off to sleep.

High up a bird wheeled and swooped, darted across the

boat and then was gone, soaring to grey clouds. A slight drizzle began to fall, fine like dust, but they did not feel this nor had they felt the mist that closed about them. Now it was slowly rising, revealing a patch of water, a greater patch, and then a wilderness of sea, black sluggish water gobbling at the bows where Father Michaels slept.

The skyline was a shadow line. The bird returned again, swooped low, tearing at silence with a rush of wings, but none heard this, already dead to sound. Only the priest heard this and opened his eyes.

"Wind," he murmured, "wind," unable to raise his head and see a bird, far out, skimming wave on wave. He did not see a bird, but a rock that grew larger to him as he watched. He opened his mouth to cry, but only air came out. The rock drew nearer still.

A wind blew up, he gave a slight shiver, his fingers closed upon the lapels of his sodden coat, he felt the wind pass down behind his back, and tightened the collar about him. His eyes were growing dim, and then he saw it was the light, now fading fast, and wondered what hour it could be.

Thinking he heard a sound he looked round, but nothing save Curtain's body moved, gently with the boat, rocking him deeper to deep sleep. Father Michaels could not see the others, glimpsed dark blots as though from a great distance, a shipped oar, and then he was staring out to sea again. Now when he looked he imagined that he saw the figure upon the rock begin to move, a hand upraised. Watching this, his fingers gripped the wood again. He felt quite certain now that this man upon the rock was speaking to him by movements of his arm. He was filled with a desire to leave the boat, to reach out and grab this hand, which he saw so clearly now, stab of whiteness rising over seas, far-stretching grey. He thought of a hand so raised while many oceans passed, he thought of a hand that was older than the world. "Great God!" he said, "it is a rock."

A sea washed over the bow and knocked him down. He sprawled, lay still. He did not know how long he lay there, but when he woke, something big and black was drawing to him, and then he cried out, "The rock."

A fisherman was standing in a boat, pipe in his mouth, waving with both hands. A sail bellied behind his short, squat figure. He wore a reefer coat. He saw the drifting boat. His own seemed so still that it might have stood upon that patch of sea through all eternity. It now began to move.

And Father Michaels saw it move, but he could not cry out again. All that he had was gone in a single cry, "The rock!" and he lay and watched the boat move down towards him. Eyes drowned in wonder, he watched it draw nearer still, the fisherman stood clear against the sky.

Father Michaels raised himself up, and saw the man grow larger still; this man come out of mist, of nothing, of emptiness, and then he saw him close and heard him shout, "Ahoy there! Ahoy there!"

The priest looked out at him, and in his eyes, his was the shape of Christ.